Where You'll Find Me

NATASHA FRIEND

SQUARE
FISH

FARRAR STRAUS GIROUX
New York

SQUARE FISH

An imprint of Macmillan Publishing Group, LLC
175 Fifth Avenue
New York, NY 10010
fiercereads.com

Square Fish and the Square Fish logo are trademarks of Macmillan and
are used by Farrar Straus Giroux under license from Macmillan.

Our books may be purchased in bulk for promotional, educational, or business use. Please
contact your local bookseller or the Macmillan Corporate and Premium Sales Department
at (800) 221-7945 ext. 5442 or by e-mail at MacmillanSpecialMarkets@macmillan.com.

Library of Congress Cataloging-in-Publication Data
Friend, Natasha, 1972–
    Where you'll find me / Natasha Friend.
        pages ; cm
    Summary: After her mother's attempted suicide, thirteen-year-old Anna goes to live
with her father and his new family, and learns to navigate the shifting loyalties of
middle school friendships.
    ISBN 978-1-250-10442-7 (paperback)   ISBN 978-0-374-30232-0 (ebook)
    [1. Interpersonal relations—Fiction.   2. Middle schools—Fiction.   3. Schools—
Fiction.   4. Stepfamilies—Fiction.   5. Moving, Household—Fiction.   6. Mental
illness—Fiction.]   I. Title.   II. Title: Where you will find me.

PZ7.F91535Whe 2016
[Fic]—dc23

                                                                        2015004689

Originally published in the United States by Farrar Straus Giroux
First Square Fish Edition: 2017
Book designed by Elizabeth H. Clark
Square Fish logo designed by Filomena Tuosto

1   3   5   7   9   10   8   6   4   2

AR: 3.7 / LEXILE: HL520L

For Toby and Heather, who get it.
And for Mieka, Steph, and Scooper, my "everything bagels."

Where You'll Find Me

CHAPTER

1

I USED TO THINK your friends were your friends no matter what, but that's not how it works. There is elementary school, and then there is middle school, where suddenly all the rules change and no one tells you how to play and the only thing you know for sure is that you are losing. Everything about you is wrong: your hair, your personality, your jeans.

Danielle Loomis's jeans, however, are perfect. When she gets up from her desk and struts across the room to spit out her gum, you can see this clear as day. Indigo, low-rise, frayed just right. I wish I could be happy for her. I wish I could be glad that this summer, when her braces came off and her boobs came in, the whole world noticed and made her popular. But I'm not glad. I just want everything back the way it was.

I'll always care about you, Anna. Those were Dani's words on September 3, outside Brickley's Ice Cream, right after she bought me a shake. *Just because our lives are moving in opposite directions and we're hanging out with different people doesn't mean I don't care.*

Seriously. Those were her words. And trust me, when your best friend since kindergarten tells you point-blank she doesn't want to be friends anymore, here is what you do: cry. It just happens, like when you get hit in the face with a ball in gym. *Wah, wah, wah,* like a baby. You can't help yourself, even when Ethan Zane and all of his low-shorts-wearing friends suddenly appear in front of Brickley's Ice Cream on their skateboards.

That was three weeks ago. This is now. English class, and we are getting a lesson on irony. *The firehouse burned down. The police station got robbed.* If Mr. Pfaff wants irony he should take a look at his seating chart, aimed to "maximize our learning potential." To my left: Loomis, Danielle, Ex-Best Friend. To my right: Zane, Ethan, King of Eighth Grade. They are stealth-texting each other under their desks. Every two seconds Dani glances over at Ethan, flips her coppery hair, and smiles. A month ago, she didn't even have a cell phone. A month ago, she would have been passing notes to *me* on a scrap of paper. Ironic much?

"Anna?" Mr. Pfaff is standing at my desk, petting his goatee. "Can you think of an example of irony?"

How much time do you have, Mr. Pfaff? I can give you a whole list. Things I find ironic:

1. An ex-best friend who used to be so bucktoothed that Ethan Zane called her the Beaver. Suddenly she can't stop smiling.
2. Teachers who think their students are learning when they are actually texting under their desks.
3. Teachers who wear goatees to look cool.
4. Facial hair in general.

Now I am remembering the mustache my father wore for his wedding and how ridiculous it looked. The whole event was ridiculous. Which brings me to:

5. Fathers.
6. Weddings.
7. Marriage vows.

"Anna?" Mr. Pfaff is waiting. "Any ideas?"

I shake my head like I'm drawing a blank. If there is one thing I've learned in middle school, it's this: keep your mouth shut. I am practically an expert.

For three days I have been staying in my father's guest room. I have been told that this room is "mine," but that's not how it feels. This is my father's new house, my father's new family. Every night, his baby wakes me up. Whimpering, crying, screeching, I hear it all. She sounds like the monkeys at the Roger Williams Park Zoo, only I don't feel sorry for her the way I do for the monkeys. The noise drives me crazy. I don't care that she is only a baby and half-related to me. I want to scream back. Instead, I jam a pillow over my head and wait for morning.

My stepmother, Marnie, is breast-feeding. She will strip off her shirt and bare all in front of you with no regard. My father thinks this is great. He also changes Jane's diapers like he's been doing it his whole life, which I know for a fact he hasn't because my mom told me. *Your father never changed a single one of your diapers.* Direct quote.

I am so glad she isn't here to see him. My mom is in the hospital, and I don't know when she's coming out. I have been told it's no one's fault, but I am the one who called 911, so do the math. Before the ambulance came, she was in bed for seventy-two hours. "Can't get up," she said every time I walked into her room. "Too tired." So I would pour my own cereal, pack my lunch, call her work and lie. *She can't come in today. She has the flu.* Even though I knew she wasn't sick—not with the flu, anyway. I'd been through this enough times, but I'd always been able to drag her out of bed before, help her into the shower.

That morning, my mom didn't even respond when I shook her. At first I thought she was asleep, but then I saw the empty Advil bottle in her hand. Her skin wasn't even a color. Her pulse was barely a pulse.

Finding my mother like that was the scariest moment of my life. But do I talk about it in my father's house? No. I sit in his kitchen, quiet as dust, while Marnie whips it out right here at the table. Sometimes when she is nursing I have to look away, I am so embarrassed. Other times I see her and Jane all snuggled up together and I want to cry. But I stay silent. Respectful. I imagine my father's house is a five-star hotel and I am only here on vacation, eating the complimentary waffles.

"How did you sleep, Anna?" The waitress smiles at me. "Were you warm enough?"

I nod my head yes.

"I hope Jane didn't wake you."

I shake my head no.

Marnie is so pretty, if she actually were a waitress she would get great tips. Long honey-colored hair. Curves in all the right places. If she were in eighth grade at Shelby Horner Middle School, she would put Danielle Loomis to shame. That is a fact. Dani would kill to be her friend.

My mother would not kill to be Marnie's friend. She

does not speak to Marnie unless absolutely necessary. She barely speaks to my father. Last year at the wedding, while I was busy being a bridesmaid, my mom was on the couch in her sweatpants, staring at the TV. That is how I found her when I got home, staring at a television that wasn't even on.

My father is oblivious. This morning, he joins me at the bus stop—a first. There is a routine to his mornings. Number one, treadmill. Then shower, shave, read the *Wall Street Journal*. Marnie makes his coffee in a to-go cup, which my mother never did. Organic roast, almond milk. Normally he would be gone before I left, but today, there he is, standing at the end of the driveway with his hair slicked back, comb tracks still in it. Blue suit. Loafers so shiny you could see your face.

Here is the conversation:

"Got everything?" he says, eyeing my backpack.

"Yeah."

"That's good."

I nod.

He takes a sip of coffee, then another. "How's school?"

"Okay."

"Good." He juts his chin at me. "That's good." He looks away, sips his coffee. Straightens his tie.

The silence is so loud. "How are broom sales?" I say. It is a bold call, making the joke my mom used to make, about him selling brooms for a living like Hansel and Gretel's dad.

Well, that was a mistake. He does not smile.

"Anna," he says.

I look up at his face—dark brows, tan skin, handsome enough for pharmaceutical sales. "Yes?"

"I'm sorry about your mother."

And there it is. The punch in the stomach, the squeeze of the heart. "It's okay," I say.

His words buzz around in my ears. *Best doctors. Psychiatric care. New drugs for depression.*

I nod and nod.

Elevactin. Just came on the market. Free samples.

Thinking about it now, I almost laugh. Because here is the irony: My mother, Dr. Frances Collette, PhD, is the school counselor at North Kingston High School. She has an advanced degree in clinical psychology from Brown. She is a trained professional in the field of mental health. And three days ago, she tried to kill herself. *The school counselor tried to kill herself.* Mr. Pfaff . . . *ding, ding, ding* . . . we have a winner!

*   *   *

Dani is trying out for cheerleading, which says it all. On my way to the bus, there she is outside the gym, fixing her hair and bouncing on her toes. She is not standing with Jessa Bell or Whitney Anderson, so the line must be alphabetical. I watch her from the end of the hall for a few minutes, then walk by. Casual, like I don't see her.

"Hey, Anna." Dani tosses her ponytail and smiles.

"Oh, hi," I say.

She has on a tight white tank top, a magenta tennis skirt, and Nikes. Gold hoops in her ears. Eyeliner. I want to walk away, but I am frozen.

"I'm trying out for cheerleading! Can you believe it?"

"Yes."

"Lauren Goldfarb broke her leg, so there's only one spot and I probably won't get it, but . . . hey—" Dani's voice drops and she takes a step toward me. "I'm really sorry."

I look at her, hoping. "You are?"

"I heard about your mom."

"Oh."

"My mom heard from Mrs. Rose . . . at Big Y or something . . . I wondered why you weren't on the bus. I guess you're staying at your dad's . . ."

Dani keeps talking, but I am not listening. Regina Rose is my mother's best friend. I have known her my whole life and I have always liked her, but now I hate her. I hate her stinking guts.

". . . my mom sent flowers to the hospital, from all of us. Tulips."

Tulips. Well, hallelujah.

"I'm sorry." Dani cringes, reading my face.

I say nothing.

"I really am, Anna. You know I love your mom."

Nothing.

"Remember that time I was sleeping over and she gave Mr. Bojangles a makeover?"

Of course I remember. Mr. Bojangles was my guinea pig. I got him for my eighth birthday. He was calico—orange, tan, and white—but, for whatever reason, my mother decided he wasn't quite colorful enough. So one night she brought out the markers and colored all of Mr. Bo's white spots green, purple, and red. He stayed that way for weeks.

"I remember," I say.

"And that time she took us to the movies and bought every kind of candy in the concession? My mother would never do that."

Fact. Mrs. Loomis is obsessed with calories.

"Your mom is so cool," Dani says.

I know, right? Fifty Advil in one sitting. Can *your* mom do that?

Sarcasm is rising in my throat like lava, but before

I can say anything, the gym doors open and Mrs. Strand steps out with her clipboard. "Jensen, Joerger, Loomis, Lustig."

"Omigod!" Dani is smiling again, a big, happy cheerleader smile. "Wish me luck, okay?"

Flash of the teeth.

Swing of the skirt.

I'll always care about you, Anna.

Gone.

CHAPTER

2

THE DAY IT HAPPENED, I made two calls: 911 and Regina. I didn't call my father. That sounds weird, I know. A girl finds her mom half-dead and doesn't call her dad? But you have to know the history. You have to know that when it comes to my mother, David Collette is not exactly president of the Emotional Crisis Management Club. Even when they were married, he couldn't deal. Escape. Retreat. That was his M.O. When my mom got depressed he would suddenly have to go on a *sales trip*, which blows my mind when I think about it. Because he was the responsible adult and I was the kid. Okay, to be fair, my mom was never as bad as she is now. And it's not like he ever left me *alone*. He always called Regina, who isn't just my mother's best friend, she's also a nurse and an awesome cook and only too happy to swoop in and feed everyone meatballs and boss my mother around until she's okay again. Regina is great in a crisis.

When the ambulance came, she took over everything. She talked to the EMS guys. She signed forms. She didn't even make me ride to the hospital. She just told me to pack a bag, and by the time I came downstairs my father was waiting for me. Even though it wasn't Wednesday. Wednesday is his day. Wednesday and every other weekend. That was the deal. Until Monday, when my mother tried to kill herself and everything went haywire and now I'm staying in the wrong house on the wrong nights, which is basically breaking the custody agreement.

Not that I ever "agreed" in the first place. I didn't "agree" when my dad left. I didn't "agree" when he got married. I didn't "agree" to any of it, which is why, ever since he moved into his new house, I have refused to sleep over. Wednesday dinners: fine. Weekend activities: fine. But no sleepovers. Until now, when I have no choice.

I get off the bus, and there is Marnie, waving to me from the front porch. Her hair is French-braided and her Siamese twin is stuck to her hip. "Hey, Anna!" Three white satin triangles glimmer on her chest.

"Hey," I say.

She picks up Jane's hand, makes it wave. "Can you say *Hey*, Janie? Say, *Hey, Anna! How was school?*" The only thing worse than Marnie's baby talk is her Delta Delta

Delta sweatshirt. She is twenty-four years old and she still thinks she's in college. She has photos of her sorority sisters taped to the mirror in her bathroom. She has yoga pants with paw prints on the butt, a big stuffed tiger on her marital bed. My father doesn't even care. "Clemson's a great school," he says. "Great football team."

Marnie opens the door for me, lets me go first. In the foyer, she takes my backpack and my jacket. I want to tell her she's not my maid, she doesn't have to do these things, but the words don't come. They pile up in my throat like rocks.

"Are you hungry?" Marnie says.

I shrug.

"I made cookies, if you want . . . or there's fruit." She is fiddling with the chain around her neck. Instead of a charm, there is her name in gold script. *Marnie.* She used to be Marnie Staples, but then she married my father, so now she is Marnie Collette. Once I heard my mom say, "Marnie Collette. Do you know what that sounds like? A stripper."

She was on the phone with Regina when she said it, sneaking a cigarette. I could tell because I was listening on the other phone, and I could hear her inhale.

"Well, Fran," Regina said, "she probably *is* a stripper."

"Ha!" my mom snorted, exhaling. "She probably is!"

She was trying to quit. Before she went into the

15

hospital she was trying really hard. Chewing the gum, wearing the patches. She even bought these hypnosis CDs she saw advertised on TV, and she listened to them constantly. *Mind over matter, mind over matter. You have the power, you have the power.*

"Anna?" Marnie is looking at me expectantly.

"Yeah?"

She holds out a plate. "Would you like a cookie?"

I would not like a cookie, but I take one anyway.

"They're carob chip." She smiles. "Your dad's favorite."

Since when? That is my question. *Since when does he like carob?*

"I want you to know," Marnie says out of nowhere, "that your friends are welcome here. Anytime. You don't even have to ask."

I nod, like I am considering this. A year ago, I actually had friends. Besides Dani, there was Keesha Soboleski. It was always the three of us: Dani, Keesha, and Anna, inseparable. Then last fall, after the divorce was final but before my dad married Marnie, Keesha's dad got a job coaching basketball in Pennsylvania and she had to move. Dani was my best friend, no question, but right now I miss Keesha more. She was so funny. She would do things like show up at your house wearing a mustache she'd made out of felt. "Who am I?" she would say. You'd guess and guess, but you would never be right because it was always someone you hadn't heard of. Burt Reynolds. Clark Gable. Keesha watched a lot of old movies. Sometimes she would make you put on a trench coat and sunglasses and walk around town with her, pretending to be Sherlock Holmes and Watson. Even if you didn't want to, you would do it, feeling like an idiot at first, but by the end you would be peeing-your-pants laughing.

I haven't laughed like that in weeks. Even now, in my father's kitchen, when Jane lets out a huge burp that Marnie thinks is hilarious, I don't laugh. I take a bite of cookie.

"Excuse my daughter," Marnie says. "She thinks she's a frat boy." She kisses Jane's cheek and coos. "Don't you, my angel? Don't you think you're a big, hairy Alpha Delta Phi?"

Jane burps again. Marnie cracks up. She snuggles Jane against her chest and kisses the top of her head.

Suddenly I am remembering this photo from my baby album. I am about Jane's age, with wild curls and a white eyelet dress. I am sitting in my mom's lap, craning my neck to look up at her, but she isn't looking at me. She is staring out the window. Her arms are hanging at her sides like dead wood. Once you see something like that, you can't unsee it. Every time you think about it your mouth tastes like pennies.

When Marnie isn't looking, I spit her cookie in the trash.

*　　*　　*

Here is what I know about my mother:

1. She is in Butler Hospital, the psychiatric hospital.
2. She is "under observation," which means the doctors are watching her every move to make sure she doesn't hurt herself. Which is what happens, I guess, when you swallow a bottle of pills. People read you loud and clear.
3. She can't have any visitors. She is too "emotionally fragile."

That is all my father will tell me except for *Don't worry, Anna, your mother is going to be fine.* Well, how does he know she's going to be fine? He's not a doctor. He's not even her husband anymore. What does he know about anything?

*　　*　　*

Six o'clock and my father is home. He is standing in the driveway, talking on his phone. I watch him from the window for a while, then go out to tell him it's dinnertime. He nods but doesn't stop talking. "Jim," he says, "I'm telling you. Rigoris is the next Viagra . . . How do I know? Because I know."

He rolls his eyes at me like we're sharing a joke. Which we are not. I have tried to joke with my father in the past, telling knock-knocks or riddles I think are funny, but he never laughs as hard as I do. Our humor just misses.

"Uh-huh." My father is nodding. "Well, Jim, that is what I would call a paradigm shift."

Paradigm shift. Benchmarking. Value added. He might as well be speaking Hindi. He is still at it when Marnie steps out on the porch looking completely different. Instead of the sweatshirt, she has on a lime-green sundress and high strappy sandals. Instead of the braids, her hair is loose and wavy around her shoulders. As soon as my father sees her he hangs up. Just like that, he's done with Jim.

"Babe," he says, staring her up and down. "Wow."

"This old thing?" she says, pouting like a model.

Marnie holds so much power. She flicks a switch in my father like nothing I have ever seen. It is a pure mystery how she does it. Once I tried walking down the hall like her, chest pushed out, hips swaying side to side. I waited for the boys to notice. Nothing, except for Kevin Callahan practically slamming me into a locker. "Watch where you're going," he said, like it was my fault.

Marnie walks inside first, followed by my father, then me. It is just the three of us for dinner. Jane is asleep in her bassinet, resting up for a night of screaming ahead.

Which I think is the worst kind of planning, but I am not the mother.

I sit at the dining room table, napkin in lap and hands on napkin. I look to see what Marnie has made. Burgers. Good. It is hard to mess up burgers. Then I take a bite and realize I am dead wrong.

"They're black bean!" Marnie announces.

I watch my father lift his burger to his mouth and chew. And chew. And chew several more times before he finally takes a gulp of water.

"Oh no," Marnie says, looking at him. Her green eyes are wide, spiky with mascara. "You don't like it."

My father shakes his head. "It's great."

"You hate it."

"Babe, I was just surprised. I thought it was beef."

"Red meat contains carnitine, which can damage your heart. It increases your risk of type two diabetes." Marnie's voice is getting higher. "It puts stress on your colon and your brain!"

Here is where I should tell you that my father loves burgers. Every Wednesday when he takes me to Denny's—the divorced dads' restaurant of choice—he gets the same thing: the Bacon Slamburger with cheese fries. But does he admit that now? No. My father gets up and walks around the table. He wraps his arms around Marnie and kisses her, full on, as though they are alone and his thirteen-year-old daughter is at a sleepover.

I take this opportunity to spit black beans into my napkin.

After the make-out session ends and Marnie is calm, my father gestures to the table. "Who needs red meat? . . . Am I right, Anna?"

I do what I am supposed to do: nod.

Marnie smiles and says there's rice pudding for dessert. Made with almond milk and sweetened with real maple syrup.

"Rice pudding?" my father repeats. Then, like I'm deaf, "Did you hear that, Anna? Rice pudding with real maple syrup!"

I know he is trying to make Marnie feel better, but please. "Wow," I say, going for sarcasm, but my voice is so low no one notices.

Marnie stands up like she is on a mission, serving out broccoli (organic!) and mushrooms (full of potassium!). When I take my next bite, I force my lips smile-ward. *Almost as good as the Shelby Horner cafeteria!*

*   *   *

I am in bed when I hear something. A soft moaning. The baby, I think. No. It's not that. The wind? It's not that

21

either. The sound gets louder and louder and I know, suddenly, what it is. Marnie and my father, doing what couples do in the dark. I know because when Dani and I were friends we used to watch this movie her parents kept hidden in their room. *9½ Weeks*. It tells you everything you need to know about sex, even if you are not old enough to know it.

Oh, this is too mortifying for words. Worse than Jane screaming at the top of her lungs. Worse than my mom crying in the bathroom, running water so I won't hear.

Thoughts flicker through my head like sparks. What if Marnie gets pregnant again? What if they need this room for the new baby? What if my mom never gets out of the hospital and the bank takes our house? Where will I go?

The questions hurt to think about, and the answers hurt more. I breathe and breathe. Even though I have never touched a cigarette, I repeat the quit-smoking mantra in my head. *Mind over matter, mind over matter. You have the power, you have the power.* Over and over, until I fall asleep.

CHAPTER

3

THE NEXT MORNING, Sarabeth Mueller flags me down.
All week she has been doing this, saving a seat for me
on the bus. It is worse than sitting alone, but I don't
want to hurt her feelings. I take off my backpack, rest
it in my lap.

"Hi, Anna."

"Hi," I say.

Sarabeth Mueller is so pale you can see her veins.
Practically everything about her is see-through. Skin,
hair, fingernails, eyebrows. There is a pink ribbon of
scalp where she parts her hair. Once, when we were
on a class trip to the beach, I saw her squirt sunscreen
on it.

"Want to know what I'm doing this weekend?"

"Okay."

I do not want to know what Sarabeth Mueller is doing this weekend. I am sure it has something to do with dolls. In sixth grade, she had a birthday party and we spent the entire time in her bedroom drinking tea and looking at her dolls. She had about a million of them, all dressed up and staring down at us from shelves.

Sarabeth adjusts the hem of her skirt. "Ever hear of Irish step dancing?"

"Um. I don't think so."

"Well, it's a traditional performance dance that originated in Ireland. I've been doing it since I was four. Saturday I have a competition."

"Cool."

I am lying so bad. I know exactly what Sarabeth is talking about because in seventh grade there was this talent show and she got up onstage and danced for the whole school. It was the craziest thing. Little Sarabeth Mueller, all alone with her white toothpick legs and her big black clogs, going like sixty. The ninth-grade boys had a field day. Dani and I sat in the back of the auditorium, the only ones not laughing.

Of course, that was last year. Now if there were a talent show, Dani would be front and center. She would be up onstage with Jessa Bell and Whitney Anderson and all those girls, shimmying around in her tube top and platform heels, making the ninth-grade boys whistle. And you'd still find me in the back of the auditorium, not laughing.

"So," Sarabeth says now, "how long will your mom be out of town?"

This is what I told her my first day on the bus, and it's not exactly a lie. My mother *is* out of town. "Not long," I say.

"Do you like staying at your dad's?"

I shrug. "It's okay."

"When did they get divorced?"

"A year ago." I am chewing on my thumbnail. I am squinting out the window, hoping we're close to school, but we're not.

"That's tough," Sarabeth says. "My grandparents are divorced. Both sets. If you ever need someone to talk to . . ."

"Okay."

I don't know why I'm saying okay. I don't even know if Sarabeth means I can talk to her or to her divorced grandparents. All I know is I need one of those school bus emergency drills. The driver presses a button and an escape hatch opens. He doesn't even have to slow down. I'll just jump.

*　　*　　*

"The sum of the angles is . . . uh . . . ninety degrees," I tell Ms. Baer-Leighton.

Ms. Baer-Leighton is drinking something brown out of a Poland Spring bottle. She takes a swallow and nods. "Yes."

I fiddle with my protractor. "So that means they're . . . uh . . . complementary angles?"

"Is that your final answer?"

Oh, I hate math so much. No teacher but Ms. Baer-Leighton makes you stand up in the middle of class like this, stuttering like an idiot while laser-beam eyes shoot holes in your back.

"No," I say. "Supplementary."

Behind me, someone sniggers.

"The first rule of mathematics"—Ms. Baer-Leighton swishes her bottle around and around—"as in life, is to trust your instincts." She takes a sip. Whatever she is drinking matches her sawed-off haircut. Also her scarf, dress, and practical pumps. Brown, brown, brown.

Your clothes tell a lot about you, Dani said once. *Jean-on-jean is a message you don't want to send. Try a pop of color. Accessorize.*

"Do you understand what I'm saying, Anna?" Ms. Baer-Leighton is looking at me, forehead shining in the light.

"Yes," I say.

She raises a fist in the air. "Confidence!"

I sit down at my desk, die a little.

*   *   *

In English Mr. Pfaff gives everyone a sheet of lined paper and tells us to freewrite for ten minutes. It's his favorite thing, freewriting. Every class he makes us freewrite, and every time my brain freezes and I can barely eke out two sentences. Sometimes I wonder if he is doing it just to torture me.

Today our prompt is "morning madness." What I really want to write is *I am mad this morning because I am being forced to freewrite*, but I know this is not what Mr. Pfaff is looking for. So I stare at my paper and think of all the other things I could tell him.

1. I am mad this morning because I heard my father and stepmother doing it last night and was too mortified to look them in the eye at breakfast.

2. I am mad this morning because I have to ride this new bus and Dani's not on it, not that she would be sitting with me anyway, but now I have to sit with Sara-beth Mueller.

3. I am mad this morning because my mom is in the psychiatric ward, also known as the madhouse. Get it? MADhouse?

Of course, there are a lot of reasons why my mother ended up in the hospital, most of which have nothing to do with me. But I am the daughter. I was there and I should have seen it coming. Because there are always signs. The way her voice sounds, or little shifts in her behavior, like forgetting to brush her teeth. Red flags. But in a way, I ignored them. I'm not good with impending disaster. I'd be the one in the middle of the tornado saying, "Don't worry, Dorothy and Toto. Really. It's just a breeze." I am the one who, instead of writing down all the bad thoughts in my head, will chew on my pencil and keep my paper clean.

Ten minutes later, Mr. Pfaff is looking over my shoulder, petting his goatee. When he talks, he lowers his voice, but it really isn't low at all. It's more like an announcement to the whole class.

"You can't think of anything to write?"

I shake my head. I can feel Dani looking at me but stare straight ahead.

"Nothing at all?"

I sink down lower in my seat.

"Why don't you stop by and see me after school and we'll talk about it?"

I nod, as though I am agreeing.

He smiles, as though he believes me.

It's official. I now hate English more than I hate math.

*   *   *

Since Keesha moved and Dani ditched me, I have no one to sit with at lunch. So I have been sitting at this random table with Sarabeth Mueller. Also Chloe Hartman and Nicole Dodd, who are obsessed with witches, and Shawna Wendall, who actually *looks* like a witch. I think it has something to do with her eyebrows, which she plucks bald and then draws over with black pencil so they're dagger-like points. Then there's this girl who just moved here from Texas. Her name is Reese and she barely says a word. She has the same three things every day without fail: sesame bagel, banana, milk. Which would bore my taste buds practically to death, but she doesn't seem to mind.

Across from me, Sarabeth Mueller has a carrot in her mouth and a pen in her hand and is scribbling away in a spiral notebook. Whatever she is writing she sure looks jazzed about, ignoring the argument heating up between Chloe and Nicole. Not that it's so fascinating. I've never read the *Complete Book of Witchcraft*, and I really don't care if it's better or worse than *Wicca: A Guide for the Solitary Practitioner.*

I glance over at Jessa Bell's table, where Dani now resides. She looks completely at home there, eating Cheez Doodles, flipping her ponytail, smiling. I actually watch her do all three at once, a skill I never knew existed. If there were a talent show tonight, Dani would win.

"What's with all the ponytail flipping?" I would ask her if we were still friends. "Are you swatting flies?" Then, "Is Cheez Doodle dust the new manicure?" And Dani would laugh. My questions would be sarcastic, but she would know I was joking because best friends always know. They read each other's mind. They finish each other's sentences. That's how it was for me and Dani, before she morphed into someone I don't know.

Dani catches me looking and I squint, pretending to read the clock over her head. I shift my gaze back to my own table, where Chloe and Nicole are still arguing, Reese is picking all the sesame seeds off her bagel, and Sarabeth is scribbling away.

"Done!" Sarabeth says, suddenly shutting the notebook and tucking the pen behind her ear.

"With what?" Shawna says, looking annoyed. Shawna always looks annoyed.

Sarabeth smiles mysteriously. "Just a little something I've been working on . . . All will be revealed in time."

Shawna looks more annoyed. Chloe tells Nicole she doesn't know crap about Wiccan literature. Reese begins tossing sesame seeds into her mouth, one at a time, like some kind of performing seal.

I can't believe this is my table.

* * *

Again, the Dynamic Duo is waiting on the porch when I get home from school. Marnie is holding an envelope.

"This came for you," she says, shifting Jane on her hip so she can hand it to me.

I see my mom's spidery handwriting and instantly feel sick. The way you do when you're in an elevator and it shoots to the thirtieth floor, leaving your stomach in the lobby.

"Anna—" Marnie starts to say, but I cut her off.

"I'm going upstairs."

"Okay." She reaches past me to open the door.

I have hands, I want to say.

"Jane and I will fix you a snack," she tells me. "Okay? Just come down when you're ready."

I nod, heading for the stairs. There's a carpet runner, maroon and green paisley, that's supposed to keep people from slipping, but it is so ugly you could slip just trying not to look at it. In my house, the stairs are polished wood, same as the floors. My mom likes natural lines, clean surfaces. Which is ironic when I think about her bedroom that day. Clothes everywhere, when she likes them neatly folded. Bed rumpled, when she likes it made. That day, the air had an unwashed smell. Sour. It makes me mad to think about. Why couldn't she just get up and take a shower? Put on deodorant and go to work like a normal parent?

*　　*　　*

I stand in my father's guest room, staring at the envelope. *Frances Collette, Butler Hospital.* "Eff you," I whisper. I should feel guilty, but I don't. Especially when I take the letter out and read it.

> *Hi honey. It's me.*
>
> *I haven't been a very good mother. I wish I could promise you that when I get out everything will be different, but I don't know if it will. All I can say is I'm sorry.*
>
> *—Mom*

It is so lame it's comical. I try to laugh, but the sound gets caught in my throat. It stays there all night, like a hair ball caught in a drain.

CHAPTER

4

MY MOTHER HATES DOCTORS. This is my first thought in the morning. *My mother hates doctors and she's stuck in the hospital.* It's like a joke without a punch line. I stare at the ceiling, remembering one time she had strep throat. How old was I? Six? Seven? Anyway, instead of calling the doctor, she tried all these home remedies: gargling with salt water, raw honey, cayenne pepper. Nothing worked. Finally, my father realized how sick she was, and somehow, because he is a pharmaceutical rep, he was able to get my mother antibiotics without her having to go to a doctor's office.

He used to love her. This is my next thought. I know for a fact he loved her, at least when I was younger, before they started fighting. They had fun together. I remember one night in third grade I had a bad dream and

I went into their room, but the bed was empty. So I went downstairs and there they were, dancing in the kitchen. No music, just my mom singing and my dad smiling and their two bodies swaying like blades of grass in the wind. And when my mom saw me, she grabbed my hand and said, "Dance with us, Anna." And I did. I know that sounds weird, but I did. I danced in the kitchen with my parents. Because that's how it was. Mom, Dad, and Anna, the Three Musketeers. The Three Amigos. For twelve whole years, that's how it was.

We used to be a family. This is my third thought, the most pathetic of all. We stopped being a family so fast my head is still spinning.

One minute you are eating Cheerios like a normal, happy kid. The next your parents are sitting down at the table with their coffee, saying, "Honey, we have something to tell you."

They are getting a divorce, they say. It's been in the works for a while. (Which is code for *everything has already been decided.* Lawyers have been met with. Custody has been arranged. They're just waiting for the paperwork.)

It's no one's fault, they say.

Relationships are complicated, they say.

This will be better for everyone, they say. You'll see.

Really? Is it "better for everyone" when your father

moves into one of those horrible apartments over by the mall, with the cheap appliances and the scratchy brown carpet? An apartment that, even though there's a pull-out couch, you point-blank refuse to sleep in, partly because you're mad, and partly because there's a lingering smell of cat pee from the last tenant?

Is it "better for everyone" when your father goes to a pharmaceutical sales conference in Atlanta and comes home looking happier than you've ever seen him? And now he's flying to Atlanta every two weeks? Because, guess what, even though the divorce isn't "official" yet, he's met someone! And suddenly, at one of your lame Wednesday-night Denny's dinners, here she is. And she's so pretty you want to puke.

Is it "better for everyone" when, surprise! Even though the divorce isn't "official" yet, they're engaged? And surprise again, you're going to be a big sister?

This all happened in a year. The divorce was final in September; they were married in November; Marnie had Jane in April; they bought the house in June. Boom, boom, boom, boom. Now here we are, September again. My mother is stuck in the hospital and I am stuck in my father's guest room, staring at the ceiling, while Jane wakes up and starts wailing. Clearly, this is better for everyone.

*　　*　　*

If I have to spend a whole weekend inside this house, I will go crazy, I realize, so I take Marnie's bike. She said I could borrow it. I ride around their neighborhood for a while, chugging up hills, flying down. As far as athletic talent goes, this is it for me. I can ride a bike. All those P.E. games—dodgeball, kick ball, volleyball—oh, I am the worst. More than once, I have literally hurt *myself* in gym class. Slammed my own knee into my nose, poked my own finger in my eye. Dani, though—she's always been coordinated. She will get that one spot on the cheerleading squad. I know it. When we were friends, we used to do Just Dance on the Wii in her basement. Dani got all the "Gold Moves." The most I got was "OK."

Without really thinking about it, I find myself riding to Dani's house. How many times have I showed up at the Loomises' doorstep unannounced on a Saturday morning? Hundreds. Something about the air in Dani's kitchen—her mom's potpourri and Lemon Pledge and whatever is baking in the oven—has always smelled like home to me. I think I just need a whiff of it.

Of course, the minute the door opens, I know I have made a mistake.

"Anna!" Mrs. Loomis says, all wide-eyed and fake-sounding. She is wearing her aerobics outfit, complete with sweatband. "What a nice surprise! . . . Girls, look who's here. It's Anna!"

I can see from where I am standing that it's not just Dani at the table. It's Jessa Bell and Whitney Anderson. And they didn't just show up, either. They are wearing pajamas and eating post-sleepover pancakes.

Like an idiot, I wave.

Three limp hands wave back.

"How are you doing, honey?" Mrs. Loomis asks, lowering her voice and squeezing my arm with her sweaty fingers.

I know what she is asking. It's not about me and Dani; it's about my mother.

"Okay," I say.

Her voice drops even lower. "How's your mom?"

"She's okay."

"Good." Mrs. Loomis smiles and nods. "That's good . . . We sent flowers to the hospital," she adds. "Tulips."

Again with the tulips.

"ARE YOU HUNGRY?" Her voice is suddenly loud, like she's trying to blast me with good cheer. "DO YOU WANT A PANCAKE?"

I force a smile and nod. "Okay."

"WELL, GRAB A CHAIR! THERE'S PLENTY!"

Mrs. Loomis gives my arm another squeeze, then hightails it down to the basement, where her workout room is. This is what Dani's mother does. Power 90, TurboFire, Biggest Loser. Exercise is her life.

I wish I could follow her down there. Or run out the door, hop on Marnie's bike, and ride away. But I can't. Whitney Anderson is waving me over, and you don't ignore Whitney Anderson. Unlike Jessa Bell, whose power comes from ignoring people she thinks are losers, Whitney is straight-up mean. Oh, she looks sweet and shiny in her cupcake pajamas, and the corners of her mouth are turned upward, but that doesn't tell you anything. I've seen Whitney in action. In sixth grade, just because my hair is dark and curly, she said it looked like pubic hair. For the rest of the year, the boys called me Pubes.

"How are you, Anna?" Whitney says, as though she talks to me every day.

"Fine," I say. I take the empty chair next to Dani, who doesn't say a word. Jessa, cool as can be, pops a bite of pancake into her mouth.

"What'd you do last night?" Whitney says.

It is not an unfriendly question. She is still smiling. But Whitney knows, and I know, and Dani and Jessa know, exactly what she's saying. *Last night, while you were home alone, the three of us were having a blast.*

I tell her I didn't do much, just hung out.

"Who'd you hang out with? Sarabeth Mueller?"

Jessa snorts into her napkin.

I force a laugh. "No."

Dani says nothing.

"Sarabeth Mueller is a mutant," Whitney says, smirking. "I swear to God, I've never seen anyone so pale in my life. Do you guys remember that time in sixth grade when she got that nasty sunburn? And it peeled all over the place?"

Jessa shakes her silky blond head. "Oh my God, gross."

"Remember Tyler Banks called her a leper?" Whitney says. "And you had to walk her to the nurse, Dee, to get aloe vera?"

Dani is "Dee" now, apparently. A new name to go with her new friends and her new personality. "Oh my God," she says. "Yeah. Aloe vera."

Suddenly she is standing. "Can I talk to you for a minute, Anna?"

I look at her face, trying to gauge what she is thinking. "Sure," I say.

"Have a good chat!" I hear Whitney call, as I follow Dani out the front door and onto the porch.

When we're alone, she turns to me. "What are you doing here?"

"I don't know," I say. Which is a bold-faced lie. I am

here because I need my best friend. And I thought if we hung out again, just the two of us, she might reconsider. *Oh yeah!* she would say. *I forgot how much fun we have together!*

Dani holds up both hands.

"What?" I say. "I just felt like coming over." Then I throw in some sarcasm. "I didn't realize you had *houseguests.*"

It's funny, but Dani doesn't laugh. "You've put me in an awkward position," she says.

"How?"

"I thought I was clear before."

"About what?"

She hesitates. "About our friendship."

"What about it?" I'm looking straight at her. There's a splotch of maple syrup on one cheek, dry skin on her lips where she always gets it.

She looks away.

"What?" I say again. I'm playing dumb and it's killing me, but I'm not about to back down now.

"We're not friends anymore, Anna!" Dani suddenly explodes. "Okay? I'm sorry about your mom, but you can't just show up at my house uninvited! It's embarrassing!"

It's embarrassing. Well, what is a person supposed to say? There is nothing left to say. My eyes can't even look at her. I grab the bike, which is propped against the same tree Dani and I once carved our initials into. *DL + AC = BFF*. Fourth grade, that's when we did it. We used Mr. Loomis's jackknife. We got in trouble, but we didn't care.

"Anna," Dani says as I grab Marnie's helmet, snap it on.

Don't look, I tell myself.

"Anna," she says again, louder. "Wait. I know that sounded harsh—"

No, I will not wait. I will hop on and pedal.

"You'll make new friends!"

Pedal, pedal, pedal away.

*　　*　　*

I find myself at Starbucks, not because I'm hungry but because I don't want to go back to my dad's. There's a boy ahead of me in line, my age, maybe older, wearing a fleece vest. His hair is sticking out around his baseball cap, blond and soft-looking. I pretend to study the pastries while he orders. *Grande mocha Frappuccino, extra whipped cream.*

The barista repeats it back. "Grande mocha Frapp, extra whip." Then, "Would you like to try one of our apple cider doughnuts today?"

"Uh, no thanks."

I open my mouth without thinking. "They're really good."

The boy turns around. Eyes the color of sea glass. Freckly nose. Cute. So cute! "What?" he says.

"The cider doughnuts," I say. "They're actually good."

"Yeah?"

"Yeah."

"So you're saying I should get one?"

"I'm saying you should get one."

He smiles at me. I cannot believe it, but he does. I know there are girls this happens to all the time, but I am not one of them.

"You won't regret it," I say.

He orders the doughnut. I am scanning my brain for what to say next when a girl exits the ladies' room, all tight jeans and leather boots.

The boy's eyes light up. "Hey," he says. "I got you a doughnut."

The girl's lip-glossy mouth twists into a pout. "I hate doughnuts. You know that." She reaches out to smack his butt.

I turn away, embarrassed. If I ever have a boyfriend, I won't smack his butt in public, I promise you that. And I will appreciate every doughnut he buys me.

*   *   *

When I get back, my dad is talking on his phone in the driveway, but Marnie and Jane are in the kitchen, waiting for me.

"What's this?" I say when Marnie hands me a bag.

She smiles. "Open it and see."

I have to give her credit for surprising me. She bought me a phone. Or, technically, my father's AmEx bought me a phone, but it was Marnie's idea. It's black with an orange case, Clemson colors, which I would not have chosen for myself, but I am not complaining. Another thing I am not doing is telling Marnie that my mother won't let me have my own phone until I'm sixteen. *Cell phone use in teenagers has been linked to sleep disorders, high-risk behavior, sexting, cyberbullying . . .* The speech goes on and on, but as far as I am concerned, it is no longer relevant. The school counselor has lost her right to vote.

"Do you like it?" Marnie says.

"Yes."

"She likes it, Janie!"

Marnie lifts one of Jane's tiny fists in the air. Today she is strapped into the BabyBjörn, facing out. She is wearing a miniature pink tracksuit with pink-and-gray-striped booties. Her cheeks are rosy and she has Marnie's emerald-colored eyes. It is sad to say that I am jealous of a baby's eyes, but I am. Mine are plain brown, same as my hair, same as my freckles. I have always thought this was part of my problem. Brown, brown, brown, just like Ms. Baer-Leighton.

"You can change the color if you want," Marnie says, but she is not talking about my looks, she is talking about the phone.

Oh, no, I tell her. I like the orange, really.

Marnie looks so happy you would think *I* gave *her* a present. "It's charged and ready to go," she says. "Do you want me to show you how to set up the address book? We can put all your friends' numbers in there."

All my friends. Right.

"Maybe later," I say. I thank Marnie and head up-stairs to the guest room. The phone is light in my hand, smaller than a deck of cards. It is the newest version, better than Dani's. But I'll bet Dani has a hundred friends in her phone already. She is one of Them now, a hoarder of likes and posts and hits and forwards. She texts with Ethan Zane in English, so of course she has boys' numbers in there, too. Her phone might not have cost as much as mine, but it is worth more.

I sit on the edge of the guest bed, staring at Marnie's present. What if I called Dani right now? Hey! I'd say. Guess what? I got a phone! But I realize that even if I wanted to call her, I don't have her number. Dani never gave it to me.

I sit on the bed, feeling like a loser. The girl with the cool new phone and no one to call. Pathetic. I get up, walk over to the dresser to shove the phone in a drawer. But as soon as I open it there is my mother's letter.

It's like a kick in the gut, the feeling. I just want her here so I can yell at her and then she can apologize. *I'm sorry, Anna,* she will say. *I'm all better now. Let's go home.*

But how can I yell at someone I'm not even allowed to talk to? The closest I can come is writing back.

I open the guest room door and walk softly through the hall. I know I should not be stealing five pieces of orange tiger-paw stationery off Marnie's bedside table, but that is what I'm doing.

I grab the paper, go back to the guest room, sit on the floor, and write.

Dear Mom,
    I will not be sending you this letter. That's the first thing you should know. I may be writing it, but I will not be sending it. So I guess there's really no point in telling you that this paper is Marnie's and I took it without asking. Or that she just bought me a phone. Do you even care? You don't, Mom, is the answer to that. You don't care. You're alone in some hospital room right now, probably staring at nothing. Even though it's the

weekend and you're supposed to be home being a mother, you're not. You don't even know what being a mother means or why a daughter might need you to be one.

It's starting to rain, if you must know. The kind of day that makes most people want to curl up on the couch with a good book. Most people. Do you remember, Mom, that time it was raining and you dragged me out of bed in the middle of the night?

YOU: Wake up, Anna.

ME: It's two in the morning.

YOU: It's afternoon in China.

ME: Mom.

YOU: It's raining, honey! It's glorious! We need to get out there!

So we went outside at two in the morning. Do you remember? We didn't even put on bathing suits, we just stayed in our pajamas and got soaking wet. We stomped in puddles and sang every song from the <u>Evita</u> sound track and you got a pail and we filled it with night crawlers we found squiggling under the street lamp. And it was fun, okay? I admit it. But come on. What kind of mother does that? What kind of mother wakes her ten-year-old up in the middle of the night and drags her out in the rain in her pajamas?

And while we're on the subject, what kind of mother sells her car and brings home a motorcycle? Dad said, Where's the Subaru, Frances? And you said, Why drive a Subaru when you can drive a Harley? He was so mad he stormed out of the house, but you just laughed and called after him, Lighten up, David! Lighten up!

What kind of mother gets a tattoo of Judy Garland on her shoulder? What kind of mother steps into traffic without looking, just to see what will happen?

I have to stop writing. I'm getting a pit in my stomach, thinking about my mom. I used to think she did crazy things because she was cool and brave and wild and rare. But I don't know anymore. I'm starting to think I had it backward. I'm starting to think maybe she did those things because she's actually crazy.

CHAPTER

5

SUNDAY AFTERNOON I am doing my homework. Well, technically, I am sitting cross-legged on the guest room floor with *To Kill a Mockingbird* in my lap, chomping on a pencil and waiting for inspiration to strike. It is hard to be inspired in this room. No desk. No posters. Nothing at all, really. Just a bed and a dresser and a straight-backed chair over by the window where I put my backpack. Walls: white. Sheets: white. Carpet: beige. I might as well be living at the Holiday Inn.

I know this is my choice. I know I could decorate it any way I want. That was literally the first thing my dad said when he showed me the room. "This is your space, Anna. Decorate it any way you want." It could be just like my old room, he said. I could have a beanbag couch.

I could have a shag rug. I could paint constellations on the ceiling and peace signs on the walls.

This isn't my space! I wanted to scream at him, scream until the ceiling cracked and the walls came crashing down.

I didn't scream, of course. I just calmly told him that this was not my house, any more than his lame bachelor apartment had been my house, and that I would not be sleeping over. Ever.

And he calmly responded, "I won't force you to sleep here, Anna. But decorating your room would mean a lot to Marnie, so just think about it."

I hated the way he said that, like Marnie's feelings mattered more. Like the things she left for me on the bed—a Pottery Barn teen catalog, paint samples from Benjamin Moore—could possibly make up for anything. *Thanks, Marnie, a Totally Trellis comforter and Aztec Lily walls will totally erase the fact that you and my dad got together a month after he left his family.*

I wouldn't do that to my mom. I couldn't. Decorating this room, moving into my father's pretty new life with his pretty new wife, would send my mom right over the edge.

Over the edge, where she went anyway. Because I couldn't stop her. Because I ignored all the signs—

No, I am not going to think about that. I am going to think about *To Kill a Mockingbird*. I open my book, pull out Mr. Pfaff's essay question. *What is Atticus Finch's relationship to Maycomb? What is his role in the community?*

I can do this. I can answer this.

But before I can write a word, there's a knock on the door.

"I'm working," I say.

Marnie pops her head in anyway. "Hi," she says, smiling. "Sorry to interrupt, but you have a phone call." She walks over, holding out the cordless. Her nails are shiny peach ovals. "It's Regina."

Crap.

I wait for Marnie to leave. She hovers in the doorway for a moment. "You okay?"

"Fine," I say.

As soon as she closes the door, I pick up the phone. "Hello," I say, all ice queen.

"Anna Banana?"

Hearing her voice, warm and deep like a man's, a picture pops into my head. Regina Rose wearing one of her favorite tent-like shirts—the yellow one with the cowboy motif—and her bangs are sky-high. Regina is a big woman. Big voice, big hair, big boobs, big, strong arms. When she pulls you in for a hug, there is no escape. I used to love getting hugged by Regina. She is warm and wobbly like a water bed, and she always smells like tomato sauce. Gravy, she calls it. I love Regina's gravy, but I will not be eating it again.

"How are you, honey?" Regina asks.

I say nothing.

"Anna?"

Silence.

"Can you hear me?"

This coming from the loudest person I know.

"Anna?" she says again. "Are you there?"

"I'm here," I say flatly.

"Good. I thought I lost you."

If only.

"How are you doing at your dad's?" she says. "Are you eating enough?" Regina thinks everyone is too thin. She cooks constantly, and I am her favorite customer. Meatballs, baked ziti, lacey Italian cookies. I have sat in Regina's kitchen a million times, eating her food. A million times, I have stuffed my face with garlic knots while she and my mom drank wine and listened to Italian opera.

Suddenly the words burst out of me. "Why are you telling everyone about my mother?"

"What?" Regina sounds surprised.

"Dani says you told her mom. In the *middle of Big Y.*"

"Oh, honey. It was hardly the middle of Big Y. It was a discreet corner. The ethnic foods section."

"I can't believe you did that. I can't believe you're telling people."

"Your mom needs all the love and support she can get right now."

"That's your idea of love and support? Blabbing her personal business to the whole world?"

"Joyce Loomis is not the whole world. She's a friend of your mom, and I thought she should know."

I snort. I don't bother telling Regina that because Dani and I are no longer friends, by the transitive property our mothers are no longer friends. I just snort.

"Okay," she says. "So you're mad at me."

I think about denying it, but I don't.

"It's okay to be mad at me. Be as mad as you want. I can take it."

"Fine," I say. "I will . . . I *am*."

"I know you are. It's all right."

Silence for a moment. Then she says, "So, okay, we've established that you're pissed at me. And we've established that it's fine that you're pissed at me. And now we need to talk about your mom."

I feel a little twist in my stomach.

"Okay? Can we do that?"

My voice comes out low. "Have you seen her?"

"Not yet. But I've been talking to her doctors. They've

been trying, based on what happened, based on your mom's history, to come up with an accurate diagnosis."

"What do you mean, *an accurate diagnosis*? It's depression. She gets depressed. You give her pills and she gets better."

Regina is the one who explained this to me in the first place—how not long after I was born, my mother developed postpartum depression. She was so sad and tired she couldn't get out of bed, so she had to go into the hospital. My dad was left to take care of me, which was not part of the plan. You know that movie about the three single guys and the baby that suddenly gets dropped on their doorstep? They're so befuddled they don't know what to do? *How do we put on this diaper? What do babies eat?* That was my dad, minus the roommates to help him, so he called Regina. I don't remember any of this, obviously. But Regina told me the story when I was in second grade, on the morning my mom was so tired she couldn't get out of bed and go to my school play. I don't think I will ever forget how it made me feel. Like my mom's depression was my fault. Like giving birth to me broke something inside of her. That's how little kids think, right? In literal terms? *I broke it; now I need to fix it.*

"It may not be as simple as depression," Regina says

now. "And the medication she's been given in the past may not have been the right medication."

"Why not?"

"Well . . . I need you to think back for me. Not about this week, when your mom was clearly depressed, but about the weeks leading up to her depression . . . What was she like?"

"What was she *like*?" I say. "She was Mom. You know what she's like."

"Energized? Excited about things? Working on a project?"

"Obviously."

This is one of the things I love about my mom. She's always jazzed about something. This summer it was guinea hens. She'd read some scientific journal article about Lyme disease and discovered that guinea hens eat the ticks that carry the bacteria. Most people would read the article and say, *Hmm, that's interesting*. But my mom springs into action. She joins the Guinea Fowl Breeders Association. She buys the wood and the wire and the nails. She digs the trench in the backyard and builds the coop and orders the eggs. And then, when the chicks hatch, she names them all after Broadway stars you have never heard of. Gertrude Lawrence. Pearl Bailey. Betty Buckley. She sings them show tunes. She paints little signs for their roosts.

"Remember the guinea hens?" I say.

Regina saw the whole thing. My mom called her when the chicks hatched. They drank champagne to celebrate.

"I do," Regina says. She starts to say something else, hesitates. Then, "What else?"

"What do you mean?"

"Do you remember any other projects—say, before your dad moved out?"

I'm tired, I realize. I don't want to have this conversation. I want to lie down on the bed, take a little nap. Wake up in a year.

"Anna. I know this isn't easy. But I need you to bear with me."

"I *am*."

"Remember the painting project?"

Regina is really starting to bug me. Of *course* I remember the painting project. I was *there*. It was the last big fight my parents had before they split up, and I was right in the middle of it.

The way it started was my mom went to some workshop on the psychology of color, and when she came home she decided to repaint the whole house. First she made a chart: rooms, moods they should create, best colors to reflect those moods. *Front hall: orange; welcoming energy. Downstairs bathroom: blue; peace and relaxation.*

She bought paint. She took all the art off the walls. She moved the furniture into the middle of each room. I was excited because my room was going to be green, harmony and stability, and because I would get to use the paint roller. My father was not excited. He thought the whole thing was a GD shit storm. He said my mother would never finish and he would have to clean up the GD mess.

I sigh into the phone.

"What?" Regina says. "Say it."

"Say what?"

"Whatever's on your mind."

"My dad was right. It was a shit storm."

"Anna."

"What?"

"Honey," Regina says softly, "that's mania. The flip side of depression. Your mom's projects? Those times when she's really, really energized and doesn't need to sleep more than a few hours? That's actually part of her sickness."

"Oh."

"It's a new diagnosis they're considering. Bipolar two."

"So, what—Dr. Amman was wrong? She's not depressed?"

Dr. Amman is a psychiatrist friend of Regina's—the one she drags my mother to whenever she can't get out of bed. My mom hates going, but Regina makes her go anyway. Because Regina is only a nurse and can't prescribe medication.

"Dr. Amman was half-right."

"How can you be half-right?" I say.

"He treated half your mom's problem, and the pills only worked to a certain extent, when she was willing to take them. The doctors at the hospital are trying to figure out which medications, in which combinations, will work to stabilize *all* of your mom's symptoms and make her feel better."

"When can I see her?" I say. "When can she come home?"

"Let's take this one step at a time," Regina says.

Who put you *in charge?* I want to yell at her. I feel a knot of craziness forming in my stomach and another one in my throat.

"This sucks," I choke out.

"She's going to be okay," Regina says. "I promise. You just need to give her time."

Time? It's been a week already. How much more does she need?

CHAPTER

6

"THIS IS WHAT I was working on," Sarabeth says on Monday morning. "Invitations!" The bus hasn't even moved and already she is handing me a card.

"Thanks," I say.

"You're welcome."

I feel a little dread, opening it. I am remembering the last Sarabeth Mueller fiesta I attended. Chamomile tea, watercress sandwiches, dolls. I am not judging. I am not saying people shouldn't like what they like, or shouldn't throw whatever kind of party they want to throw. It's just—okay, here it is—I am reading the first line: *Calling all women of substance!*

"Women of substance?" I say.

Sarabeth smiles. "You, Shawna, Chloe, Nicole, and Reese. It's a famous-women-in-history party! You can come as anyone you want. Pocahontas. Cleopatra . . . Marie Antoinette . . . Anne Frank."

Anne Frank? I am thinking. How could Anne Frank go to a party? She couldn't go anywhere, not even to school. Not even to the fruit cart to buy an apple. I was blown away by that book. I felt all scooped out inside. For weeks afterward, I felt that way.

"It doesn't have to be Anne Frank," Sarabeth assures me. "Whoever. You can even pick someone who's still alive, like Hillary Clinton."

"Oh."

"So . . ."

"So?"

"Are you free on Saturday night?"

It takes me a minute to realize she's not joking. She actually thinks I have a life.

"I don't know," I say. "I have to ask my dad."

I still haven't told Sarabeth about my mother. I have not told anyone about my mother. The only people who know are the people who found out on their own or the people Regina blabbed to.

"So you'll call me?" Sarabeth says.

"What?"

"You'll call and tell me if you can come?"

"Uh . . . yeah."

"Do you have a cell?"

"Yeah."

"Here," she says, reaching out her hand. "I'll plug in my number."

*　　*　　*

After third period, Mr. Pfaff finds me at my locker. He says he thought we had a plan to meet after school last week.

"I must have forgotten," I say.

"No problem," he tells me. He's free now.

I think about lying, saying I have class, but Mr. Pfaff is holding my schedule right there in his hand. He knows I have study hall.

"Why don't we take a walk?" Mr. Pfaff gestures down the hall like it's a country lane. The bell rings, and all the little worker bees fly off to class. The only noise in the hall is the squeak of Mr. Pfaff's loafers.

"I have no trouble thinking of things to write," I blurt.

"Okay."

"I can write fine."

Mr. Pfaff doesn't say anything, but out of the corner of my eye I can see him nodding. I keep my head down. Tan-and-green-speckled tiles, the same flooring that covered the halls of my old elementary school. The same flooring that Dani threw up on in second grade. For the record, I'm the one who got the nurse. I'm the one who rubbed Dani's back when she cried and I'm the one who told Tommy Markowitz to shut his trap when he called Dani a crybaby. Maybe I should remind Dani of this. Some things are worth remembering.

"Anna," Mr. Pfaff says.

I look up.

"I know there's a lot going on at home."

"You do?"

"Yes," he says. Then, "I'm sorry about your mother."

"How do you know about my mother?"

"We had a team meeting," Mr. Pfaff explains. "Last week. Your father, your teachers, the school counselor . . ."

Well. There is not much that can humiliate you more than grown-ups discussing your private business behind your back. I remember my dad mentioning a meeting, but I thought that was just about switching buses. I didn't think he would tell them *everything*.

". . . Her name is Mrs. Ramondetta. She's easy to talk to. I think you would really—"

"No," I bark. I have stopped walking, halted right here in the hallway. "No school counselor."

"Anna."

"My *mother*'s a school counselor."

Mr. Pfaff starts to put his hand on my arm, then stops himself, like he just remembered the rule. *No PDA at Shelby Horner Middle School.* No hugging! No back rubs! No touching of any kind! It's a big joke with the students, but the teachers take it seriously. Mr. Pfaff's hand flies to his goatee instead. Why did he have to grow that thing? It's like roadkill on his chin.

"We're all here for you," he says. "I know that sounds . . . canned. But listen, we really are."

Oh, this is the worst. The worst! I shift my gaze to the wall.

"You don't have to write me a novel, Anna. You just have to . . . show a little effort in class. I can't grade a blank paper. I need *something* . . . Anna?"

It kills me to look at him, but I do. His eyebrows, two fuzzy black caterpillars, are raised.

"Fine," I say.

"Fine?"

"I will show more effort."

"Great!"

Mr. Pfaff looks so pleased I should probably feel guilty for lying, but I don't. I am just glad the conversation is over.

*   *   *

The day drags on. I eat lunch in silence, which is easy because Chloe and Nicole do all the talking. Apparently there is more than one kind of witch. There are your Gardnerians and your Alexandrians. Your Eclectics and your Reconstructionists.

Chloe and Nicole argue. Can you call yourself a true Wiccan if you're not from a lineaged coven?

"Who cares?" Shawna says. "It's all bullshit."

I want to agree with her. But agreeing with her would mean joining the conversation. Instead I focus my attention on the center table, where Ethan Zane has dropped an ice cube down Dani's shirt. I watch her squeal and pretend to get mad. It reminds me of one of those advice columns she used to tear out of magazines and read to me on the bus.

Dear Seventeen,
     This guy Ethan always snaps my bra and whacks me on the butt with a lunch tray. I really like him. Do you think he likes me? What should I do?
          Signed, Snapped and Whacked in Rhode Island

Dear Snapped,
     Squeal and pretend to get mad. If he keeps doing it, he likes you.

I know I shouldn't be watching. Dani's life is no longer any of my business; she made that perfectly clear. But sometimes you can't help yourself. It's like the car wreck on the highway. You don't want to look, but your head just spins around anyway.

"She should pants him."

I look at Shawna. She is watching the same scene I am. "What do you think, Anna? One quick yank for all womankind?"

Pantsing. I haven't heard that expression since sixth grade, when the boys were constantly pulling each other's shorts down. They'd surprise attack from anywhere. The cafeteria, the playground, the bus line. I'm not saying it wasn't funny. It was. I laughed a lot in sixth grade. Now, I can barely open my mouth to take a bite of sandwich.

When I do, it tastes like sawdust.

*   *   *

After lunch I have Practical Life. Don't ask me why, but this class is mandatory for Shelby Horner eighth graders. Once a week, my Practical Life "team" gathers in the industrial arts room to learn such exciting skills as how to wash clothes, how to balance a checkbook, and how to sew on a button. Today . . . are you ready for this? . . . we're learning how to make a grilled cheese sandwich.

Apparently, most thirteen-year-olds in Westerly, Rhode Island, would not survive a week without their parents.

Apparently, I am the weirdo who can.

I have been cooking and doing laundry since elementary school. Only child, working parents, everyone pitches in. It's not like it's so hard. Jeans dirty? Throw in a load of darks. Need a snack? Fire up a Hot Pocket. They never treated me like a baby; they treated me like an equal. Which is why it's so strange now, having Marnie hovering around, bringing me clean underwear, making sure I'm eating all four food groups. It's like she's auditioning for the mother in the school play. *I have a mom, remember?* I want to tell her, every time she does something nice. *I don't need your help.*

"All right, everyone." Mrs. Beckwith claps her hands. She gestures to the stove in front of us. "This is a gas range."

She starts describing how it works. *These are the burners. These are the burner control knobs. As you turn the knob, you determine just how much gas reaches the burner. The higher the number, the more gas is released.*

Really? Wow. That's amazing.

If my mother had a burner control knob, I could set her however I wanted. If, say, she started staying up too late, watching QVC, and ordering a bunch of wineglass necklaces, I could turn her down to 6. If I found her in the bathtub with a washcloth over her face, listening to "Anatevka" on her boom box, I'd turn her up to 4.

Talking too fast? Down a notch.

Monotone voice? Up a notch.

If my mom had a burner control knob, maybe my dad never would have left. He could have kept her at a fun level. A 7, maybe. Like she was for those parties they used to throw. Neighborhood parties, birthday parties, holiday parties. When she was up, my mom was the queen of parties. She loved to drink and laugh and sing. We had a karaoke machine that my dad gave her for Christmas one year, and she always set that on the back deck. I felt proud watching her karaoke. It didn't matter what kind of song it was—Bon Jovi or Neil Diamond or Weezer—my mom could nail it. She could literally sing anything. There was this one party . . . I can't remember what it was for. But she wore her long black hair straight down, and red lipstick, and a flower tucked behind one ear. She sang "Pour Some Sugar on Me." And she was so good. She was standing on the picnic table in her dark jeans and high heels, legs a mile long. Everyone at the party stopped what they were doing just to watch her. And do you know what my dad did? . . . I'll never forget this . . . he got up on the picnic table and started rocking out next to her. He played *air guitar*.

God, I can't believe it now. Those were my *parents*. I remember the awe of watching them, a little kid at a grown-up party. Looking back, my mom was probably drunk and my dad was just trying to keep her from falling off the picnic table, but I didn't know that then. I only thought, *Those rock stars are my parents*.

If my mom had a burner control knob, I would set her for that night.

I'd keep her right there, on 7, for as long as I could.

AFTER DINNER, Regina calls again.

"Good news," she tells me. "Your mom is being released on Friday."

"She is?"

"She is. I'll be picking her up in the morning, and she'll stay with me until she's ready to get back to a regular routine. The doctors think—"

"Wait," I say. "She's not coming *home*?"

"Not yet, no. I've taken some time off work. She'll be staying with me until—"

"*Why?*"

"Your mom is extremely vulnerable right now, honey. She needs rest. She needs good food and moral support and TLC."

"She's got me!"

"Anna," Regina says in the exaggeratedly slow voice of a kindergarten teacher. Which she is not. She is a nurse. "Your mother is not ready to go home yet. I know this is hard for you to hear, but you're going to have to trust me. She needs a support system that is bigger than you."

I don't say anything.

"Okay, honey?"

Again, I say nothing. I feel sick.

"I'll call you on Friday," Regina says. "Let you know how she's settling in, okay?"

"Okay."

I am such a bad daughter. The relief is just pouring out of me.

*　　*　　*

All week I am waiting for Friday. Waiting for Friday and dreading Friday. Waiting for Friday and dreading Friday. One minute I'm excited, the next I'm nauseated. I wonder how my mother will sound on the phone. Will she use her monotone voice? Will she try to fake it? I can always tell when she fakes it.

In English, it's freewriting again and, as usual, nothing comes out of my pen. From the look on Mr. Pfaff's face when I hand in my blank paper, I can tell that he is not impressed. The writing prompt was, "What is something you're optimistic about?" But all I could think was, *My mom is coming home on Friday.* Well, not "home." She is going to Regina's and I have no control over that. I have no control over anything. Part of me wants to scream and another part wants to just lie down in my bed, pull up the covers, and stay there all day. My real bed, in my real house, where I have slept since I was two. Only I don't know if I will ever sleep in that bed again. *I guess I'm scared to feel "optimistic" about anything, Mr. Pfaff, is the problem.*

I look at him. *Ask me what I'm thinking. Ask me and I'll tell you.*

But Mr. Pfaff doesn't ask. He just takes my paper.

*   *   *

In study hall, I feel Shawna Wendall watching me. She always sits at the same desk, in the far left corner of the room, and I always sit in the far right. Usually we ignore each other, but today I feel her staring. When I look up, she arches her penciled-on eyebrows at me. A what's-up-with-you? look.

I shrug.

Shawna scowls.

Wow. I am disappointing people left and right.

I look down and try to read my science book. After a minute, a wad of paper hits me in the head. When I look up again, Shawna waves me over. I make my way to the other side of the room and pull up a chair, quick, so Mrs. Sasso won't yell at me. We're allowed to talk in study hall but we're not supposed to change seats.

"What's wrong with you?" Shawna demands.

"Nothing." *Everything*, I want to say.

When she unzips her purse, I notice that her finger-nails are painted black with tiny white skulls. They match her crossbone earrings.

"Are you going to this stupid thing on Saturday?" she asks, pulling out Sarabeth's invitation and flinging it down on the desk.

"I don't know," I say.

My dad said I could go. I told Sarabeth I was coming. But now I picture my mom, calling from Regina's. *Honey*, she says, *I feel fine. I don't want to stay here. Pack your bags. I'm coming to get you.* And then she picks me up and we drive home and everything is—poof!—back to normal.

"I'm not going if you're not going," Shawna says.

I look at her.

She rolls her eyes. "Whatever. I don't care if you don't go. I'll have more fun without you."

"Oh yeah?"

"Yeah," she says. "You're a real ray of sunshine."

"You're a real picnic yourself," I say.

She smirks, which is the closest thing I've ever seen to Shawna Wendall smiling. Out of nowhere she says, "Let me see your fingernails."

"Why?"

"You bite them, don't you?"

"No."

"You do. I can tell. You're a nail-biter."

"I am not."

She narrows her eyes at me.

I fold my hands across my chest.

"Oral fixation," Shawna says. "Patient is unconsciously obsessed with her mouth and always needs to be sucking or chewing something. Jolly Ranchers, pencils, fingernails."

I make a scoffing sound, even though I do love Jolly Ranchers and all my pencils have tooth marks on them. "Are you a psychologist?"

"Amateur."

"Fine," I say. "I bite my nails. So what?"

"So I'll paint them."

"I'm not into skulls and crossbones."

"What are you into? Rainbows and lollipops?"

Shawna Wendall is by far the weirdest, most sarcastic girl I have ever met. Everything she says is caustic.

"What's wrong with rainbows and lollipops?"

"Nothing. If you're a bubble-gum princess."

"You don't know me at all," I say.

Shawna makes a face. "Who says I want to?"

I stare at her in disbelief.

"I'm just doing this out of the goodness of my heart." She reaches into her purse and pulls out a bottle of silvery black nail polish. "*Gobsmacked*. Best color ever."

I have no idea why she chose me, or why I'm letting her, but somehow, in the middle of fifth-period study hall, I find myself getting a manicure from Shawna Wendall.

*   *   *

After school I go straight to my father's computer and Google "oral fixation." There are over two million entries. It's hard to know where to begin, so I just click on the first link. *In psychology, the "oral stage" is a term used by Sigmund Freud to describe the child's development during the first year and a half of life, in which an infant's pleasure centers are in the mouth.*

"Doing something for school?" I hear Marnie ask.

I quickly put my hands over the monitor. "It's private."

"Oh," she says. "I'm sorry."

I can tell from her voice that she is hurt, and I feel

bad for snapping at her, but why does she have to be looking over my shoulder every two seconds, and opening doors, and making snacks?

"I just came to see if you wanted a snack," Marnie says.

"I don't."

"I'll leave you alone, then."

Good, I think. *She's leaving.* Then, because I feel like a jerk, I say, "I'm looking up oral fixation."

"Oral fixation?" Marnie turns back around.

"Yeah," I say. "Why? Have you heard of it?"

Her face lights up. "Oh my God, totally! I was a psych major at Clemson!"

Great. I have unleashed the Tiger.

"The infant who is neglected," Marnie reads over my shoulder, *"or overfed in the course of being nursed might become an orally fixated person."* She laughs. "Wow. I actually remember that! I used to highlight my psych textbooks with, like, a million different colors. I had this whole system . . ."

While Marnie is taking a trip down Tiger lane, all I can think about is those words. *The infant who is neglected or overfed in the course of being nursed might become an orally fixated person.*

"She never nursed me."

"Pardon?" Marnie says.

"My mother. She never nursed me when I was a baby.

She says it didn't work for her, but I don't think that's true. She just didn't want to."

"Oh, Anna. I wasn't—"

"It's okay," I say. "It's not your fault I bite my nails."

"If it makes you feel any better, Jane will probably be orally fixated, too. She's always on the boob!"

This makes me feel worse, actually, but Marnie keeps going.

"Just wait. When she wakes up from her nap she'll be all over me . . . Anyway, lots of children are bottle-fed, and they turn out fine. It doesn't mean their mothers love them less just because they don't breast-feed."

What about mothers who try to kill themselves? Do they love their children less? This is the question I need answered—the thought I can't stop thinking. If she loved me, how could she have done what she did?

But I can't ask Marnie. She has stopped talking and is just standing there on the rug. Awkward, like she doesn't know what to do without a baby in her arms. She loves Jane so much. She can't wait for her to wake up from her nap. A mother like that couldn't possibly understand.

*   *   *

My father gets home late. It's the third night this week he's missed dinner. I can hear him and Marnie arguing in their bedroom—not the words, but the tone. He and my mom fought a lot before he moved out, but this is the first time I've heard him fight with Marnie.

Afterward, he knocks on my door.

"How are you?" he says.

"Fine."

"How's school?"

"Okay."

He nods, clears his throat. He looks uncomfortable standing in the doorway. He is still wearing his suit.

"You talk to Regina?" he says gruffly.

"Yeah."

"She's picking your mother up on Friday?"

"Yeah."

"She'll be better soon." He says this with confidence, like he's talking to someone from work. My mom getting better is a *guaranteed outcome*.

I nod.

"You know Regina," my father says. "She'll have your mother kneading bread dough as soon as she walks into the kitchen."

He is joking, I think. Or harshing on Regina. It's hard to tell.

"What were you and Marnie fighting about?" I say.

"We weren't fighting."

"Is it because you came home late?"

"No."

"Is it because she made kale again?"

"No." My father smiles a little.

Marnie has been cooking a lot of kale lately. Also Swiss chard. She is into "superfoods." Most of what she cooks tastes really weird, but at least she's trying. My mother never cooked me anything but scrambled eggs, and I don't think that counts. Her idea of dinner is Mr. Wong's takeout or cornflakes. You never know what's coming. One night she's too tired to feed you and the next night she bursts through the door with a French baguette under each arm, an eighty-dollar bottle of wine for her, Orangina for you, and fifteen types of gourmet cheese. When I remind my father of the Parisian picnic smackdown—the night last spring when he came home and found us eating Gruyère on the floor, and he screamed at my mom for her inability to serve a proper meal—he practically bites my head off.

"This is *nothing* like me and your mother. *Nothing*." Then, more gently, "Marnie and I weren't fighting, Anna. We were discussing."

"Oh," I say. I wait for him to tell me what, exactly, they were discussing. But he doesn't.

"Do you understand the difference?"

"Yes." The difference is he hates my mom but he loves Marnie.

"It's important to communicate," my father says. "Communication is the cornerstone of any good relationship."

Right, I want to say. *Which is why we have such an awesome father-daughter bond. We communicate so well.*

*   *   *

When I get off the bus on Friday I go straight to the kitchen. I don't even bother taking off my backpack. "Hi, Anna," Marnie says, holding up a plate. "Rice chips and salsa?"

"Did my mom call?" I say.

She shakes her head. For a moment I see pity in her eyes and I hate her for it.

"I can make you something else if you want," she says. "Apple and peanut butter? . . . Yogurt?"

"You can't *make* yogurt."

I sound like one of those snotty teenagers on Nickelodeon. I hate myself. Also, you *can* make yogurt. I saw it on the Food Network.

Marnie should call me on it: my tone and my yogurt facts. Maybe if she got mad at me for once, I would respect her more.

But she doesn't.

Later, my father takes us out to dinner. I wonder what

Marnie told him. *Your daughter is a little snot.* Or, *Why don't you distract her with chimichangas so she forgets that her own mother can't be bothered to call her?*

When I was little, I used to play this game with myself at restaurants. After I ordered, I would go to the bathroom. I would take my sweet time. While I was washing my hands, I would picture my food waiting for me on the table. Then, when I came out, poof! There my burger and fries would be, like magic.

Tonight I do a new version of this. *When I get back to my dad's, a message will be waiting for me. When I get back to my dad's, a message will be waiting for me.* I think this all through dinner.

And when we get back, a message *is* waiting for me. But it's not from my mother. It's from Regina.

My mom is fine, the voice mail says. She's exhausted. She'll call me tomorrow.

Fine. Exhausted. Tomorrow. I lie in bed repeating these words to myself until they stick in my brain. It's stupid, I know, but it's like a mantra. The more you say it, the more you convince yourself it's true.

CHAPTER

8

ALL DAY I WAIT for my mother to call. Nine o'clock, nothing. One o'clock, nothing. Four o'clock, Jane is on her third nap and my dad is out mowing the lawn. I am watching *Cupcake Wars* and pretending not to listen for the phone.

It's the final elimination round. The flavors are Chai Spice, Apple Fritter, Mocha Lava, and Peach Bellini. It's a repeat, and I already know who wins. Apple Fritter. I am just trying to distract myself.

"Hey," Marnie says, suddenly plopping down next to me with Jane in her lap. "Look who's up from her nap!"

"Hey," I say.

"Say *hey*, Janie. Can you say *hey* to Anna?"

I can't deal with them right now. If Marnie strips

off her shirt and starts nursing, I will seriously leave this couch.

"We love *Cupcake Wars*," Marnie says, kissing the top of Jane's head. "Don't we, baby?"

It's all I can do not to snort. "I thought you didn't eat sugar."

"I try not to eat *refined* sugar, but there are lots of ways to bake without it. Applesauce, coconut cream, even roasted vegetables . . . they can all be used as sweeteners."

"Oh, God," I mutter. "Kale cupcakes." I grab the remote and turn up the volume, hoping Marnie will take the hint.

She does, at least until the commercial. Then she says, "Hey. Don't you have a party to get ready for?"

I shrug.

"No?"

"I can't go."

"Why not?"

"I don't have anything to wear." This is BS, of course. Regina has been back to the house twice to pack up clothes for me. Twice, she has dropped duffel bags on my father's porch so I would have everything I need. Marnie knows this, but she doesn't call me on it.

"Come with me," she says, standing up and propping Jane on her hip.

"Where?"

"Just come."

I follow her upstairs and into the master bedroom. Marnie has an outfit for every occasion, it seems. Her side of the closet is packed, and she keeps pulling out random things. A feather boa. Leather chaps. An old-fashioned nurse's cap. A nun's habit.

"Okay," Marnie says. "Do you want to be Mae West? Annie Oakley? Florence Nightingale, or . . . Mother Teresa?"

I stare at her.

"Women's studies minor," she says, by way of explanation. She holds up a tennis dress. "Billie Jean King?"

I stare at the pile in her arms.

"Frat parties," she says. "We dressed up for everything."

I point to the cone-shaped bra in her hand. "What was *that* for?"

"Madonna party. Want to try it on?"

"God, no."

She laughs.

Marnie is very good at clothes. I'll bet she had a million Barbies growing up and each one had her own closet.

"Oh my God!" Marnie suddenly exclaims. "Yes!" She pulls out a small, brimless hat with a chinstrap. She pulls out a garment bag. "Yes, yes, yes, yes, yes!"

"What?" I say.

"Jackie O!" She turns to Jane, who has been sitting in her bouncy seat this whole time, gumming her fist. "Right, Janie? Is Jackie O not perfection?"

"Jackie O," I repeat.

"Jacqueline Kennedy Onassis," Marnie says reverently. "She wasn't just a Kennedy, she was a fashion icon."

"And she wore that silly hat?"

"This *silly hat*," Marnie says, "is a pillbox. It is one of the lasting images of the 1960s." She perches the thing on her head and checks herself out in the mirror. "I had a great time in this hat."

"At what?" I say. "A 1960s party?"

"A mile-high party."

"What's a mile-high party?"

"Never mind that," Marnie says. "Let's just say that the Theta Chis dressed as pilots and the Tri Delts dressed as sixties flight attendants."

"Oh."

Marnie turns to Jane again. "*Service with a smile, mile after mile*, right, sweetie pie?"

Jane gurgles.

I'm confused. "Jackie O was a flight attendant?"

"No," Marnie says, tossing everything on the bed. "But the hat works . . . Okay." She claps her hands. "First things first. The coif. Have you ever blown your hair straight?"

I shake my head.

"Ohhh. This is gonna be fun."

Moments later, I find myself on a swivel chair and Marnie is going to town on me. Squirt bottle, hair dryer, straightening balm. At one point Jane starts to squawk, so Marnie scoops her out of the bouncy seat and sets her in my lap. "Hang there, sweet girl. We're doing your sister's hair."

Your sister's hair. I don't know why the words make the breath catch in my throat. I know, technically, that Jane and I are sisters. But hearing Marnie say it feels . . . I don't know . . . real.

"See, Janie?" Marnie says. "We use the *round* brush. Someday, when you have hair, we'll use the round brush on *you*."

I look down at Jane's head. Nothing but fuzz there, really. But so soft. I touch it a few times while Marnie works.

"Ta-da!" she says finally, whirling the chair around so I face the dresser mirror.

"Wow," I say quietly.

"See?" Marnie says. She holds a hand mirror behind my head so I can get the full effect. There is not a frizz to be found. My hair is a clean, smooth sheet, swept to one side and flipped up at the ends.

"Just wait," Marnie says. "This is only phase one." She reaches into a dresser drawer and pulls out a shiny black case. "Now we even out your complexion."

She tells me to close my eyes.

I do.

She dabs a wedge-shaped sponge all over my face. Dab, dab, dab. Dab, dab, dab. Then she fluffs everything with a big feathery brush. "Translucent powder," she explains, "to set our canvas . . . Okay, you can open."

I open.

Marnie takes a step back, squinting at me. "Good. We're going for the doe-eyed look. Minimalist."

Jane wiggles in my lap. She reaches out her arms for Marnie.

"Not yet, sweetie pie. Still working here."

Jane whimpers, but when I lift my hand to stroke her cheek she grabs hold of my finger and starts gumming away on it.

Marnie laughs. "You're her teething biscuit."

It is kind of gross, having someone slime all over your hand, but Jane seems happy so I don't stop her.

"Close again," Marnie says. "And relax. This part will take awhile."

I close my eyes, sit back in the chair while Marnie "preps" my eyelids. She explains each step to me. Concealer. Primer. Matte shadow: light for the lid, dark for the crease. She is onto the liquid liner when the phone rings.

"Keep your eyes closed," Marnie says. "I don't want anything to smudge."

I hear her walk across the room, pick up the phone. "Collette residence. Marnie speaking."

Silence.

Then, "Oh, of course. She's right here . . . Anna? . . . It's your mom."

My eyes fly open.

Marnie is touching my shoulder, handing me the phone. "We'll give you some privacy," she whispers, lifting Jane off my lap, walking across the room, and closing the door behind her.

"Mom?" I say.

"Anna?"

"I thought you'd never call!"

I am so happy to hear her voice, but as soon as she hears mine she starts to cry, and once she starts she can't stop. "I'm sorry," she moans, over and over until I can't stand it. "I'm sorry, I'm sorry, I'm sorry."

"Mom." My chest tightens. "Mom, it's okay. Mom. Stop."

But she doesn't stop.

I want to say, *I know you're sad, but please, Mom, don't try swallowing a bottle of Advil again. Because if you try it again, next time it might work.*

"Mom? . . . Mommy?"

Regina gets on the phone, acting like it's no big deal. Like my mother sobbing in the background is nothing. "What's on tap for the weekend, Anna?" she booms. "Got any big plans?"

I start to tell her about Sarabeth's party, but I can't. "I thought she was better," I say, trying not to cry. "Why did they let her leave the hospital if she's not better?"

Regina doesn't talk for a moment, which is rare.

"It's complicated, honey," she says finally. "The new medicine doesn't kick in right away. It needs time to work . . . Think of it like a pair of glasses. Bipolar distorts the way your mom sees things . . . Does that make sense?"

"No."

"The right medication, like the right pair of glasses, can make her see clearly. It just takes time to find the perfect lenses. For your mom, it may take weeks. Even months."

"Months?" I choke, feeling the tears build up behind my eyeballs. "I have to stay here for *months*?"

"Honey. The doctors think—"

"But my mom has primary custody. I'm supposed to be with *her*. That was the agreement!"

"I know it was," Regina says calmly. "But these are extenuating circumstances. Your mom needs you to be strong right now. She's not going to get better if she's worrying about you. Can you do that, Anna? Can you take one for the team?"

I swallow. Say yes. Hang up.

Then I curl myself into a ball on my father's bed, bury my face in Marnie's feather boa, and dissolve.

At some point, Marnie knocks on the door. She asks if I'm okay.

"No," I tell her.

"Do you want me to come in?" she says.

"No."

"Do you want me to get your dad?"

"Definitely not."

*　　*　　*

By the time I come downstairs, it's six fifteen. I walk into the kitchen, where Jane is sitting in her high chair and my dad is spooning something into her mouth. As soon as he sees my puffy, miserable face, he stops. He does what I knew he would do: he starts blaming my mother.

He swears. He paces. He threatens to call her up right now and give her a piece of his mind.

"It's not her fault, Dad," I finally say, repeating what Regina told me. "She can't control it."

"Like hell she can't," my father says, reaching for the phone.

"Dad. It's brain chemistry." If anyone should understand that, it's him. Doesn't he sell pharmaceuticals for a living?

"Really, David," Marnie says. "What are you going to do? *Yell* at Frances for being depressed?"

My father looks from me to Marnie and back to me. He slams the phone down and runs his fingers through his hair, hard. I watch as it gets spikier and spikier, and then he growls like some kind of pterodactyl. My dad is *growling* and Marnie is staring at him like she's never seen him before in her life.

"David," she says slowly. "You need to calm down. You're acting crazy."

"*I'm* acting crazy?" he says.

"Yes."

"*I'm* acting crazy? Do you know how much crazy I had to put up with, living with that woman? Do you? *Fourteen years.* Fourteen years of crazy!"

He's ranting about my mom and I can't stand it. All I want to do is cover my ears and scream *Shut up! Shut up! Shut up!* because she is still my mom. He got to trade her in for a new wife, but I can't trade her in for a new mother. She's all I have. And she's sick. And I'm scared. And I feel like, if I'm not careful, the fear could eat me alive.

"Stop," I whisper, slumping against the wall. "Please stop."

"David," Marnie says. Sharply this time. "Take a walk. Cool off. And while you're at it, pick up some almond milk. We're running low."

My dad storms across the kitchen, slams the door behind him.

Marnie takes a deep breath, lets it out. Then she walks over to me. "I'm going to hug you now, okay?"

And I let her. Even though I don't want her to. Sometimes you just don't have the energy to argue.

*　　*　　*

"One must not let oneself be overwhelmed by sadness." This is what Marnie tells me on the way to Sarabeth's party. She is quoting Jackie O. Marnie has been president of the Jackie O fan club for the past hour, ever since she sent my father out to buy almond milk and led me back to their bedroom to fix my makeup.

Jackie O is class.

Jackie O is poise.

Jackie O is dignity.

"Harness her spirit," Marnie says now, as we sit in her VW Bug outside Sarabeth's house. I am in the back, next to Jane. The sky is dark, but I am wearing Jackie O's signature sunglasses to cover my bloodshot eyes. "She never let the dreariness of life drag her down," Marnie proclaims.

I'm not Jackie O! I want to shout. *I'm a thirteen-year-old girl with a suicidal mother, you idiot! Don't diminish my feelings!* Marnie is so wrapped up in the pillbox hat she is missing everything.

"Hey," Marnie says softly, turning around to look at me.

"What?"

"I want you to have fun tonight."

"I don't know if I can." My voice cracks as I say the words. And Marnie hears the crack, and I know she is trying to think of the right thing to say. But there is no right thing.

I get out of the car before she can even try.

CHAPTER
9

MRS. MUELLER OPENS THE DOOR. She has long straight hair like Sarabeth's, but it is reddish and her skin is not nearly as pale.

"Who do we have here?" she says.

I clutch Marnie's vintage purse to my chest. All I want to do is leave.

"Jackie O?"

I nod. Never have I been less in the mood for a party.

Mrs. Mueller whoops. "Sarabeth, you've got to see this! Jacqueline Kennedy is here!"

I glance over my shoulder, but Marnie is already backing out of the driveway. There is nowhere to go but in.

"Well?" Mrs. Mueller says, striking a pose in the foyer. She flips her hair over one shoulder. "Who am I?"

Tinted aviators, black turtleneck, flared jeans. I have no idea.

"Come on," she insists. "American feminist? Political activist? Founder of *Ms.* magazine?"

I shake my head.

"Take Your Daughter to Work Day? . . . Surely you've participated."

"God, Mother," Sarabeth says, stepping into the hallway. "Don't accost her. No one under the age of forty knows who Gloria Steinem is." Sarabeth grabs my arm. "I'm sorry. She gets carried away."

I nod.

"You look great, Anna. Wait until everyone sees you. They're all in the basement." Sarabeth leads me through the hall and down the stairs. "I'm Amelia Earhart, by the way. I found this bomber jacket on eBay, and the goggles—would you believe a *garage sale*? Three bucks."

Sarabeth is in hostess mode, chatting away, but I haven't said a word. Not one. My throat has that tight, clogged feeling, and I'm afraid of what will happen if I open my mouth.

"Hey, guys," Sarabeth says, leaping from the last step onto the carpet, "look who I found! Jackie Kennedy!"

It's quiet down here. Everyone is sitting on the two plaid couches against the wall.

"Hey, Medusa," Sarabeth says, "how would you like to turn Jackie Kennedy to stone?"

Shawna snorts, which is her signature greeting. Otherwise I would not have known who she was. Her whole face is covered in green and gray paint. She has black circles under her eyes and bloodred lipstick. A dozen rubber snakes have been woven into her hair. She's wearing a bedsheet toga. Rope belt. Gaudy gold bracelets and gold flip-flops. Even her feet have been painted green. For someone who didn't want to come to this party, she sure has gone to a lot of trouble.

"And this is the Moon Goddess of Wicca . . ." Sarabeth says, gesturing to Chloe, who is wearing a flowy white nightgown. "And the Moon Goddess of Wicca . . ." She gestures to Nicole, who is also wearing a flowy white nightgown.

Of course. Of course they're both moon goddesses. I'd love to snort like Shawna, but I don't have the energy.

"And Emily Dickinson," Sarabeth says, pointing to Reese, who is wearing a plain black dress with a frilly collar. "Doesn't she look authentic?"

I nod, vaguely remembering a picture from our seventh-grade poetry book.

Reese jerks her chin at me. "Did you know Emily Dickinson wore nothing but white after her father's death?"

I shake my head.

I have mastered the art of silence. This happens sometimes, after I've gotten emotional. I go into mental hibernation. Not deliberately. My brain just powers down for a while, until it can recharge. Because dealing with my mother takes all the voltage I've got.

Here in Sarabeth's basement, I don't care what anyone thinks, so I don't even try to snap out of it.

"Are you going to wear those sunglasses all night?" Shawna is sneering at me with bloodred lips.

I shrug. Maybe I will. Maybe I'll wear these sunglasses for the rest of the year. For the rest of my life.

"Okay," Sarabeth says, clapping her hands together. "I'm hungry. Are you guys hungry?"

Everyone shrugs.

"I'll take that as a yes," she says. "Back in a jiff!" Sarabeth races up the basement stairs.

With our hostess gone, everyone is quiet again, until the two moon goddesses start going at it.

"I thought you were coming as the Crone Goddess," Nicole says.

And Chloe says, "Why'd you think that?"

"Um, because you *told* me? Quote, 'I am going to Sarabeth's party as the Crone Goddess,' unquote?"

Chloe shrugs. "I couldn't get the look right."

"Seriously?"

"What?"

"Spray your hair white? Draw on some wrinkles? Carry a cane? You couldn't pull that off?"

"No," Chloe says. "I couldn't."

"Why not?" Nicole says.

"I couldn't find a cane."

"How could you not find a cane? You live in the woods. Grab a stick."

These two could keep going forever. They argue as if they care about the subject, but really I think they just like arguing.

"Who gives a shit?" Shawna finally says. Nicole and Chloe both stop and stare at her.

"Well, that's rude," Nicole says.

"Yeah, and it's superpolite to have inane arguments in front of people at a party."

"Vittles!" Mrs. Mueller calls from the top of the stairs, saving us. She and Sarabeth are on their way down with food. "Get your vittles here!"

"Mom," Sarabeth says. *"Vittles?"*

"What's wrong with vittles? Vittles are snack foods."

"You're dorking out."

"Oh no!" Mrs. Mueller rolls her eyes as she lowers a tray onto the coffee table. "A dorky mother!"

"Ignore her," Sarabeth says, putting down a bottle of Coke and a bowl of chips. "She's trying to be cool."

"Yes," Mrs. Mueller deadpans. "I'm trying to be cool. And hip. And *hep*. A hepcat."

"Mom," Sarabeth moans. "Don't you have somewhere to be?"

"What's that?" Mrs. Mueller grabs Sarabeth and tickles her under the arms. "You want me to *stay*? You want me to hang out in the basement *all night*? So we can talk about boys and bras and *feelings*?"

At first Sarabeth shrieks and tries to pull away, but after a minute she's laughing and tickling her mom back. They're having one of those mother-daughter moments. Or what I imagine a mother-daughter moment might be. I personally have never had a tickle fight with my mother. Watching Sarabeth and her mom, you can tell that they bug each other and love each other at the same time. They tease, but there's humor behind it.

Watching them makes my stomach hurt.

I have to go to the bathroom.

*   *   *

When I come back there's music playing—a mix Sarabeth has made for tonight. "I Am Woman" and "Girl on Fire." "Beautiful" and "Stronger" and "Roar." All this female empowerment has shut everyone up. Or it's the

Cool Ranch Doritos and M&M's they're shoving into their mouths.

I am relieved about the music. Now I don't have to talk. I can just sit on the couch and stuff my face.

At some point, "Crazy Dreams" comes on. And suddenly, out of nowhere, Shawna starts to sing. And her voice is clear and sweet. It is the total opposite of her personality and snake hair. For a moment, I am so surprised I don't know what to do with the food in my mouth, so I spit it into my hand.

I glance over at Sarabeth and she's smiling. Now she's standing up on the coffee table and starting to Irish step, which is weird because this song is not remotely Irish, but somehow it works.

Chloe and Nicole stand up and start floating around the basement in their flowy nightgowns. And now Reese joins in, but she's not singing or dancing; she's beatboxing. Tongue clicks and throat taps, bass and drums.

I watch in silence this group that has materialized. A Greek monster, an aviator, a poet, and two Wiccans. And I want to cry. Because I love this cheesy song, and they do, too. And I want to be a part of it.

I used to sing all the time. When we had the chorus elective in fifth and sixth grades, I had solos in all the concerts, not because I had such a great voice, but because I had what Mr. Potter called "chutzpah." I didn't worry about what anyone thought. I just loved how the music felt coming out of my mouth.

I want to feel that way again. I want to sing into my hairbrush, drum on my dashboard, shake the walls of Sarabeth's basement with my fearless dance moves.

But I can't. If I open my mouth, the floodgates will open. And nobody likes a crybaby.

CHAPTER
10

I CALL REGINA on Sunday night to see how my mom is doing. She starts by deflecting the question. How am *I*? she wants to know, all booming and cheerful. What did I do this weekend? What is my father feeding me?

But I keep pushing, and when the truth comes out, Regina's voice gets really soft, and the softness scares me more than the words. "I won't lie to you, honey. She's battling."

Battling. I picture my mother in a camouflage jacket and combat boots, driving a tank.

"I'm afraid she might try to hurt herself again," Regina says. "But I'm not going to let that happen. I'm going to stay with her, twenty-four/seven, until she's out of the woods."

After I hang up the phone, I lie in bed picturing my

mother in one of those old war movies, sliding along the underbrush on her belly. *See how hard I'm trying?* she says. *It's not easy to get out of the woods.* There are leaves in her hair, a little smile on her lips.

But in the next scene she's dead. Gun to the temple. Boom.

I can't sleep. I can't get that image out of my head.

*   *   *

On the bus in the morning, Sarabeth is still buzzing about her party. How great were everyone's costumes? How much fun was that, singing together? Who knew Reese could beatbox? As usual, she keeps talking, even though it's a one-way conversation. Why is it so hard for me to form words and push them out of my mouth? Why do I feel like I'm underwater? My mother's voice runs through my head, an endless loop. *Can't get up. Too tired. Can't get up. Too tired.* Well, I'm tired, too, Mom. Did you ever think of that?

"Are you okay?" Sarabeth asks finally.

"I'm tired."

"It seems like more than that. Not just today. You seemed down at my house, too."

I wasn't expecting this. I don't want to start unloading my drama, not here, not to Sarabeth Mueller.

"It's just my dad's baby," I say. Which isn't exactly a lie. "Her room is right next to mine and she's up all night crying."

"Your dad's baby?"

"My half sister, technically."

"I thought you were an only child."

I glance at her. "I was."

"Remember third grade?" she says. "We did those family trees? You and I were the only ones without siblings."

"You remember third grade?"

"I loved third grade. Everyone was friends then."

The way she says it, I know she's including me in "everyone." It's kind of a naked comment, and I'm not sure how to respond. Then this memory pops into my head: a bunch of girls playing Chinese jump rope on the blacktop behind the jungle gym. Sarabeth winding the elastic around her skinny ankles.

"Chinese jump rope," I say.

She smiles. "Yeah. And four square. You were really good at four square."

"I'm horrible at sports."

"Really? You won all the time in third grade."

The bus pulls up to the circle and we're awkward for a moment. This is where I usually take off, speed walking ahead to my locker. I'm about to do it again when it hits me.

"Was I mean to you? After third grade?" I am remembering the names people used to call her. Casper the Ghost. Albino. Powder. X-ray.

Sarabeth hesitates. "Not really. Not directly. You just kind of . . . drifted away with Danielle and Keesha. And I just kind of . . . drifted the other way."

I'm picturing icebergs.

"Anyway." She shrugs. "We're back."

Sure of herself. That's how she sounds. I think, *How are you so weirdly confident?* But I find myself walking off the bus with Sarabeth Mueller, all the way to our lockers.

*   *   *

Dani made cheerleading. I know because there is a big banner on the wall outside the gym: football players' names in blue, cheerleaders' names in gold. "Danielle Loomis," it says, right there for all the world to see.

My heart is heavy in gym class. My legs are heavier. Chloe stands on the other side of the badminton net from me, shaking her head, laughing. "You're allowed to move your feet, Anna." Nicole isn't in our gym class, so Chloe has no one to fight with about witches. She is almost normal. If normal means missing every birdie that comes her way. I'll serve it to her, and she'll make one of those dramatic, grunting leaps that professional tennis players make, and whiff, missing the birdie completely.

"You're allowed to make contact, Chloe," I find myself saying.

"I'm going for style points."

"You've got style all right."

"Look at this arabesque," she says, lifting one leg and doing another remarkable whiff.

"Wow. Thanks for the breeze."

Mrs. Strand is not amused. "Ms. Hartman," she says to Chloe, "save the fancy stuff for ballet class." She demonstrates ready badminton position: wide base, racket centered.

Chloe nods. She squats and bounces up and down, showing how ready she is. Then, as soon as Mrs. Strand turns her back, she does a flying leap, this time with her tongue out.

"Nine point two," I tell her.

"Is that all?"

"You didn't point your toes. Major deduction."

Chloe laughs. And I don't know why, but I leave gym feeling less like I swallowed a wrecking ball.

CHAPTER
11

IT'S BEEN TWO WEEKS since I've seen my mother. She has used up all her sick days at work, and it doesn't sound like she's getting any better. The good news, Regina tells me on the phone, is that my mom qualifies for a three-month medical leave for "restoration of health." Regina has filled out all the paperwork and everything has been approved.

"How is that good news?" I say.

"It means she can focus on getting well without worrying about work."

"But she's *not* getting well."

"It doesn't happen overnight, Anna."

"Yeah, well it hasn't been one night. It's been two weeks."

"I know how long it's been."

Regina sounds annoyed. With *me*. Like it's my fault she volunteered to take my mother in. Like it's my fault the medicine isn't working.

"What do the doctors say?"

"They say to be patient, Anna. She's in a holding pattern."

A *holding pattern*? Airplanes flying around in circles, waiting for clearance? It is another stupid metaphor. My mother can't get off Regina's couch, let alone fly. She won't even eat, Regina says. If she won't eat, how will she ever have the energy to get off the couch?

*   *   *

MondayTuesdayWednesdayThursday. School is a blur. I feel like I'm sleepwalking. In math, we have an angles quiz and I can't even hold up my pencil. Ms. Baer-Leighton leans over my desk and whispers, "Do you want to go to the nurse and lie down, Anna?"

Her breath smells like cough drops.

"It's okay," she says gently. "You can make this up later."

So I go to the nurse. I lie on the cot with the crinkly paper. I close my eyes.

*   *   *

Friday afternoon, eighth period, we have a pep rally. With cheerleaders. Of which Danielle Loomis is now one. I find myself on the bleachers watching Dani jump around in her blue-and-gold skirt, shaking her blue-and-gold pom-poms. I am not filled with school spirit. I don't know what I'm filled with. Dani doesn't stop smiling, not for a second, and part of me thinks she's faking it, but another part thinks she is actually happy.

S is for super!
U is for unique!
P is for perfect, 'cause you know we're sweet!

Shelby Horner cheerleaders have a passionate need to tell the world how great they are, and now they have to show the world how flexible they are by twisting their bodies into the letters *S* and *H*.

"All they need is an *I*," a voice mutters in my ear, "and a *T*."

I know instantly it's Shawna Wendall. I'm not sure how she got here, since we're supposed to be sitting by homeroom, but when I turn my head she is beside me, baring her teeth. "How much Cougar pride are you feeling right now?"

"None."

"Liar," she says. "You want to be out there cheering."

"No I don't."

"Yeah you do. You want your voice to be heard. You want to sound your barbaric yawp all over school."

I shake my head.

"Just like at Sarabeth's house. You were dying to get up and sing with us. You were on the edge of your seat."

"Yeah," I say, not because I'm agreeing but because I don't have the energy to argue. "You got me."

Before she can respond, the bell rings.

"TGIF, Cougar fans!" one of the ninth-grade cheerleaders whoops into her megaphone. "Come cheer on our boys tonight as they take on the Wolfpack under the lights!"

I can't get out of here fast enough. I grab my backpack and make my way down the bleachers, through the swarm of bodies.

"Hey," Shawna says.

She is still beside me. Why is she still beside me?

"Want to hang out? Go to Teavana or something?"

I look at her. "You drink tea?"

"Yeah. So?"

"You don't look like a tea drinker."

"What do I look like?"

I shake my head.

"No, really," Shawna says. "I want to know."

But I don't answer. Maybe later I will tell Shawna how her plucked-out, drawn-on eyebrows don't do her any favors, but right now I am too tired.

Shawna stops talking. She must have taken the hint. She doesn't seem mad, just quiet—walking along beside me, her messenger bag bumping against her leg. We make it to the buses, which is a relief. All I want is a window seat so I can rest my cheek against the glass.

"It's a compulsion," Shawna blurts just as I'm getting on.

"What?"

"My eyebrows."

It's the first time she's mentioned them. I don't want to miss my ride but something in her voice makes me step back down.

"Trichotillomania," Shawna says quietly. "It's an impulse-control disorder. I don't do it on purpose. I just . . . pull them out."

I glance at her.

"It's okay. I know I look weird."

"You don't look weird," I lie.

"Anna," she says. "Come on. You think I draw them like this by mistake? I *own* this look. I could glue on fake ones and look 'normal' "—she scratches quote marks in the air—"but this is my choice. This is me."

109

I don't know what to say, so I nod. I'm still nodding when my bus pulls away.

"Sorry about that," Shawna says.

"It's okay," I tell her. "I can walk."

"Is your house close?"

"I'm staying at my dad's, in town."

She nods. "Divorced?"

"Yeah."

"Mine, too . . . Remarried?"

"My dad is."

"Bummer."

"Yeah."

We're awkward for a moment. Then a big black car pulls up.

"This is me," Shawna says.

I am bug-eyed for a minute. "Is that a limo?"

"Town car," she says. "My dad likes to impress people. Are you impressed?"

"Kind of. Yeah."

"You want a ride?"

I shake my head. "I'll walk."

"All right, then."

She gives me a little punch on the shoulder. "Stay gold, Ponyboy."

I choke on my spit when she says that. I have read *The*

Outsiders exactly fourteen times. "That's my favorite book!"

She rolls her eyes. "Of course it is."

I return the shoulder punch, harder than intended. Shawna looks surprised, but then her mouth twitches. "Don't make me take you down, Collette."

"I'd like to see you try."

She looks completely different when she smiles.

*   *   *

A weird thing happens when I get home from school. My cell phone rings. At first I don't even realize what the sound is. I think it's the TV because that's what I'm watching. Then it hits me. I unzip my backpack and pull out the phone.

"Hello?" I say.

"Hey. It's Sarabeth."

"I know," I say. I don't bother telling her she's the only one who has this number, so who else could it be?

"Want to go to the game tonight?" she says.

"What game?"

"The football game. Cougars versus Wolfpack."

"I don't think so," I murmur.

"My mom said she'd drive us."

"That's nice, but—"

"Shawna's coming.

"*Shawna's* coming?"

Sarabeth laughs. "I promised she could make fun of the cheerleaders."

"Huh," I say.

"Come on. It's *Friday Night Lights.*"

"*Friday Night Lights,*" I repeat. This rings a bell. Did I see the movie?

"It's gonna be a great game. The Wolfpack was nine-and-oh last season, and we were eight-and-one, but our offensive line is faster."

Apparently Sarabeth is a football fan. Who knew?

"I don't know if I can go," I say.

"You can go!" Marnie calls from the kitchen.

Either she has bionic hearing or she's been listening on one of Jane's baby monitors. Either way it's annoying. I picture a night of Marnie hovering over me, asking if I want a snack.

"I can go," I tell Sarabeth.

*   *   *

By the time we get there, the bleachers are packed. The band is playing.

The cheerleaders are lined up along the track, shaking their pom-poms and bouncing all over the place. *S-P!* They shout in unison. *I-R! . . . I-T! . . . YOU GOT SPIRIT? . . . LET'S HEAR IT!*

Dani has her hair in two braids, shot through with blue and gold ribbons. I watch her do a straddle jump. Her toes come all the way up to touch her fingertips. She is so high.

Shawna elbows me in the ribs. "What did the cheerleader's left leg say to her right leg?"

"I don't know."

"As if they've ever met."

"Ha, ha."

Sarabeth, Shawna, and I squash together on one tiny stretch of bleachers. There's an electric energy in the air, a smell of popcorn and fall, but I can't enjoy any of it. There are moms everywhere. Sporty moms in Shelby Horner sweatshirts. Designer moms in 7 jeans and Uggs. Crunchy moms in flannel. There are moms laughing, moms texting, moms drinking coffee from paper cups. Everyone else is watching the football players; I am watching the moms. I am thinking, *What if she never gets off the couch? What if she keeps refusing to eat? What if Regina goes out for milk and leaves her home alone? What if she tries it again?* I keep checking my phone, to see if Regina has called.

"Why do you keep checking your phone?" Shawna says. "Are you a CIA operative or something?"

She is wearing the anti–Shelby Horner uniform: all black, from hoodie to combat boots.

"No."

"FBI? Mafia? . . . Drug dealer?"

I shake my head, tuck my phone back in my pocket. I am not in the mood for jokes. I am sitting here, surrounded by school spirit, but I don't feel it. I'm missing something. I'm missing my mom.

"Hey," Sarabeth says, taking a break from the cowbell she has been ringing. I can't believe she brought a cowbell. "You okay?"

I nod. I can feel Shawna looking at me, too. I can feel the tears pressing against my eyeballs, but I won't let them fall. I am like the little Dutch boy with his finger in the dike, holding back the flood.

What would I even say? *No, actually, you guys, I'm not okay? My mom is depressed? My mom has bipolar disorder? She tried to kill herself and I'm afraid she may try it again?*

I don't want to say any of these things. Not out loud.

At some point in the third quarter, Shelby Horner finally scores a touchdown. Everyone jumps up, screaming like maniacs. Except for me, because my finger is still in the dike. And Shawna, because she is anti–school spirit. Then the Wolfpack scores. Then, with nine seconds left on the clock, Shelby Horner scores again, and everyone jumps up and screams even louder because we won. Shawna glances at me, and our eyes lock, and she grabs my arm and pulls me to my feet.

And the band is playing and the cheerleaders are leaping and Sarabeth is banging on her cowbell, and Shawna is growling and scratching the air like a Cougar. I know she is doing this sarcastically, but it actually catches on and a bunch of people around us start doing it, too. For a moment I forget all about my mom and it feels so good. But the next moment I feel awful. Because how can I be jumping up and down at a football game when she is stuck to Regina's couch? What kind of daughter am I?

CHAPTER
12

MY FATHER AND MARNIE are fighting again. It's a stupid fight. My father has stepped out of his post-treadmill shower and there are no clean towels. This does not compute with his Sunday-morning routine.

"Just use the towel you used yesterday," Marnie says.

"I don't want the towel I used yesterday. I want a fresh towel."

"Well, I don't have one for you."

"Why not? Is the washing machine broken?"

"No. I just haven't kept up with the laundry."

"Well, do you think you could do a load today? Could you squeeze that into your busy schedule?"

Marnie storms out of their bedroom. I watch her bang open the laundry hamper and start tossing dirty clothes all over the floor. "Here!" She hurls a towel at my father, who is standing at the top of the stairs in his boxer shorts, dripping wet. "Do your own laundry!"

I watch the whole thing through a crack in the guest room door.

I watch my father try to smooth things over. He is a bumbling idiot. He has no idea how to say "I'm sorry," because he and my mother never apologized to each other. It is pitiful to behold.

"I'll go out after breakfast and buy more towels," he says, missing the point so completely I think he's joking.

He is not.

Marnie can barely look at him.

Jane wakes up and starts screeching.

"Great," Marnie says. "Now you woke the baby."

The tension is so thick I almost wish it were a school day so I had somewhere to go.

*   *   *

Later, I overhear Marnie on the phone. "I used to have a life," she says. "I used to be fun. I used to *do* things. Now I clean. And cook. And get spit up on. I don't even recognize myself."

Silence for a moment. Then, "I know, Harp."

Harp. Harper, from the wedding. Marnie's maid of honor. She's about six feet tall and lives in Atlanta.

117

There's another silence, a long one. I wish I could hear what Harper is saying, but that is the problem with cell phones. Eavesdropping is only 50 percent effective.

"Believe me," Marnie says, "the thought has crossed my mind."

What thought? I wonder. *Hiring a cleaning lady? Leaving my dad?*

"I miss college," Marnie says.

*   *   *

My father comes home victorious. He has towels! He presents the Macy's bag to Marnie like it's a woolly mammoth he clubbed himself and dragged back to the cave just for her.

"Are you serious?" Marnie says, peering into the bag.

"What?"

My father looks surprised. He expected a gold star.

"Are these ROY G. BIV?" She starts pulling out towels, one after another. Lemon yellow. Kelly green. Ruby red. She turns to me. "What do you think, Anna?"

"Wow," I say.

"It's the Hotel Collection," my father tells us. "Micro-cotton. I didn't know which color to get so I got one of each."

Orange, I think. *That's what color you get.* How has he not noticed that all the towels in this house are orange?

Marnie is laughing now. Literally every hue of the rainbow is represented on the kitchen counter. My father does not find this amusing.

"I was *trying* to do something *nice*."

"Oh, are these for me?"

"They're for both of us."

Marnie stops and looks at him. "David. You do realize you're just giving me more towels to wash."

"Why are you turning this into a laundry issue?"

"Because you made it a laundry issue. This morning. When you basically told me it's my *job* to provide you with fresh towels."

"You're the one who stopped working," my father practically shouts. "I didn't force you to. You *chose* to. You wanted to stay home and be a mom!"

"A mom to Jane, not a mom to you."

My father's face is red. He is staring at Marnie like he cannot believe she just said that.

"Anna?" Marnie turns to me. "Could you please go check on Jane? I think I hear her crying."

No, she doesn't. She's just trying to get me out of the kitchen. Which is fine with me.

* * *

119

The Fourth Annual Pharmaceutical Sales Training and Development Conference in Atlanta, Georgia: that's where my dad met Marnie. I know because they took turns telling the story at the rehearsal dinner. She was fresh out of college, working her first job. He was a panel presenter, fifteen years in the biz. Yeah, that's right. She was twenty-three, he was thirty-nine. Do the math.

You could call it love at first sight; they do. The way they tell it, they locked eyes in the exhibition tent and couldn't look away. My dad walked over to Marnie's table and took one of her free samples. They talked, they laughed, they had drinks, they fell in love in a single weekend.

I remember seeing him when he got back. I remember he took me to Denny's, and we both ordered Bacon Slamburgers. He told me he'd met someone, and he made some joke about "chemical attraction." He wanted me to be happy for him. But I wasn't happy, of course I wasn't. Even though I knew the divorce was almost final, there was a tiny part of me that was hoping my dad would change his mind and come home. And now I knew he never would. Marnie was a new beginning for him, but to me she felt like the end of everything.

I wanted to hate her. She was too pretty. She was too young. When we went out to dinner the first time, she ordered a garden salad and unsweetened iced tea. She made my father smile. Because she was so, so adorable. Marnie was the opposite of my mother in every way. And I loved my mother. And so I took it upon myself to point out, in the middle of our first dinner, that Marnie had a big, ugly blob of spinach stuck in her teeth. When she went to the bathroom to get it out, my dad shot me a look.

"Be nice," he said.

"I *am* being nice," I told him. "I was doing her a favor."

"I know what you were doing."

"What was I doing?"

"You were trying to embarrass her."

"No I wasn't."

When Marnie came back from the bathroom, she said, "Thanks, Anna."

I looked to see if she was being sarcastic, but she was smiling. With her spinach-free teeth. Like I actually did her a favor. Which made me want to hate her even more. Because she was so nice.

* * *

In the great green room . . .

Jane keeps patting the book. Pat, pat, pat. Pat, pat, pat. So I read it again. I have been up here for at least twenty minutes. I don't know if my dad and Marnie are still fighting—or "discussing," as my father would say—but I am in no rush to find out.

Reading *Goodnight Moon* reminds me of this random trip my dad took me on when I was little, to some children's museum. I can't remember where it was, but I remember there was an exhibit made to look exactly like the room in the book. With the fireplace, and the mouse, and the two little kittens—everything. There was even a black rotary telephone, and I remember I kept trying to call my mom, but she wouldn't answer. All I got was a recording. Some lady reading *Goodnight Moon*. I actually started bawling in the middle of the great green room. My dad took me out to the car and gave me a pack of Life Savers to make me feel better. Butter rum Life Savers. I ate the whole roll. Funny what you remember.

*   *   *

It's the middle of the night and I can't sleep. I try all the tricks: cleansing breaths, tranquil images, sheep. Nothing works.

I check my phone. Two twenty-six, which means only four more hours until I have to get up for school. Which means another day of sleepwalking ahead. Another day of freewriting. Another day of cheerleaders in the halls. I am tired just thinking about it. I should sleep.

I check my phone again. Two twenty-seven.

Crap. I will never sleep.

I get up, tiptoe down to the kitchen, flip on some lights. The house is too quiet. I fill a glass with water and stand in the middle of the cold ceramic floor, listening to nothing.

Nothing.

I wonder if this is what my mother feels, like a house in the middle of the night. Black and silent. Bottomless. I think, *My mom is alone in the dark and no one can get to her.* Not me. Not Regina. Not the doctors. My chest tightens at this last one. Because if the doctors can't help her turn on the lights, who can?

I am lost in these thoughts when the glass slips out of my hand. I don't know how it happens, but it does. It hits the floor and shatters. When I bend down to pick up the pieces, I cut my finger. It's pretty deep, too. It stings, and my heart speeds up when I see the blood. But I don't get a Band-Aid or anything. I just stand there, watching the blood drip onto the floor. Drip, drip, drip. Drip, drip, drip. It's the weirdest feeling, watching the blood fall, like I've been carrying around something heavy for days, but now my body is getting lighter. And lighter. And lighter.

I think about bending down and picking up another piece. So I do. I hold it gently between my fingers.

"Anna?"

I jump.

"I heard something . . ." Marnie says, standing there in her nightgown. "Oh my God. Are you *bleeding*?"

"Yeah. I broke a glass. I was trying to pick it up."

"Don't move," she says. "I'm going to get you some shoes."

I hold perfectly still.

When Marnie comes back, she slides my feet into a pair of her flip-flops. She takes my arm. "Come over to the sink."

"I'm sorry." My voice doesn't sound right.

"Don't be sorry." Marnie runs the water until it's warm. She sticks my hand under the faucet. "I'm going to fix you up, okay?"

I nod.

Marnie pats my hand softly with a towel. She pulls a first-aid kit out of a drawer. Ointment. Bandage. Direct pressure. She's a regular ER doc. "Come sit with me on the couch," she says.

I look around at the floor. "But what about—?"

"We'll clean that up later."

Marnie turns on a light in the living room, and we sit together on the leather couch under two fleece blankets.

Everything is quiet for a minute and then she turns to me. "Anna."

"Yeah?"

"Are you okay?"

"Yeah."

Marnie's eyes are serious. "I need to ask you something and I need you to be honest. Can you do that?"

I nod.

"Did you cut yourself on purpose?"

I hold very still.

"Anna?"

I shake my head.

"You didn't cut yourself on purpose?"

"No," I say. My voice is calm, but my heart is pounding. "I didn't. It was an accident."

Marnie sighs. "Good."

"What if I said yes? What would you do?"

"Then . . . I'd get you some help."

"You mean—like my mom?"

"Yes."

"I'm not her," I say.

"I know."

"I would never try . . . I would never do what she did."

"Good."

"I'm just really . . ."

"Tell me," Marnie says.

"I don't know."

"Worried about her?"

"Yeah . . . and I can't sleep. Like at all."

"Oh. Yeah." Marnie yawns. "Sleep."

"I'm so tired."

"You know, Anna—"

"I know, I know. Wait until I'm a mom with a newborn, and I'm getting up every two hours to nurse."

"I wasn't going to say that."

"You weren't?"

"No. I was going to say . . . let's get out of here."

I look at her.

"I'm serious. I think we need a change of scene. I know *I* need a change of scene. My sorority sisters are dying for me to come visit them in Atlanta, and I think we should go. Just the two of us. Girls trip."

"When?"

"Now."

"Now?" This is something my mother would do— take off on an adventure at three a.m.

Marnie smiles. "Well, not this second, obviously. But as soon as we can get ready. We need to pack. And I need to buy tickets . . ."

My mother would not think about packing. She would not reserve seats.

"I need to make a list for your dad, for Jane . . ."

"You're not bringing *Jane*?"

"Don't you think your father can take care of her for a few days?"

"Do *you*?"

"Yes. He has a flexible job. He can work from home."

"What about school?" I say.

"I'll email your principal."

"I don't know. It's just—"

"Anna, this is how spontaneity works. You have an idea and you roll with it. You work everything out as you go. That's what makes it fun. You just . . . decide you're going to do something and you do it."

She seems so sure of herself. Confident. This is Marnie, I remind myself. This is not my mother.

"There's only one question you need to answer right now . . . Do you want to go to Atlanta?"

"Yes. Yes. God! Marnie?"

"Yeah."

"It's okay if you change your mind . . . if you want to, you know, bring Jane along."

"This is just you and me."

"Okay."

I pull the fleece blanket into myself. Squeeze. My heart is beating hard again, but it's a completely new feeling.

CHAPTER
13

"YOU'RE REALLY GOING?" It's the next morning and my father is standing on the front stoop, holding Jane.

Marnie and I are standing in the driveway, holding suitcases. "It's only for three days," she says.

My father walks down the steps. He looks bewildered. Plus his hair is sticking up and he is still wearing his bathrobe. It's a very strange look for him.

This scene reminds me of all the times he went on sales trips, and I was the one standing on the front stoop. I didn't like being left. I hated it, actually. I never knew how my mother would act when he was gone, for starters. And it wasn't the family life I wanted. I wanted a dad who came home every night with a smile on his face. I wanted the three of us to wake up every morning and eat waffles together. Maybe we'd go for a bike ride. Maybe we'd play slapjack.

"I'm sorry about the towels," my father says now.

"I know." Marnie pats his cheek.

"Call me from the airport," he says. "And when you land."

The taxi driver opens the door for us. "Bye, Dad," I say.

"Bye, Anna." He squeezes my shoulder.

It's a weird kind of role reversal, a *Freaky Friday* moment.

Marnie gives Jane a hundred kisses. "Have fun," she says to my father. Then, sliding in next to me, "This is the best thing for him. He has no idea."

* * *

At the airport, Marnie does the weirdest thing. She buys doughnuts. Six of them: two glazed, two jelly, two powdered sugar.

"What are you doing?" I say when she orders.

"I'm hungry," she says. "Aren't you hungry?"

"Yeah, but . . . don't you want fruit or something?" I point to a tray of apples on the counter.

"Screw fruit. I need sugar."

This is something my mother would do—buy doughnuts for breakfast. But she wouldn't buy six, I tell myself. She would buy six dozen. She wouldn't buy milk, either. She'd buy Dom Pérignon.

After Marnie pays, we walk over to gate 37 and sit down. She opens the bag. "Dig in," she says.

I take a glazed.

"Oh my God," Marnie moans when she's bitten into a powdered sugar. "This is the best thing I've ever tasted."

She is a new Marnie: Adventure Marnie. Adventure Marnie eats junk food and talks with her mouth full. She wears no makeup. Her hair is scraped back in a ponytail. Her lips are ringed with white.

"Here," I say. I hand her a napkin. When she wipes her mouth, bits of powdered sugar float to the ground like snow.

*　　*　　*

"We have *In Touch*," Marnie says, reaching into her bag. "We have *People*. We have *Us Weekly*."

We are midflight. We have our plastic cups of Coke. We have our Cape Cod Potato Chips and our cellophane-wrapped sandwiches. Marnie won't have to cook for three whole days. I wonder if she's excited about that. I wonder what my dad will eat while we're gone. I wonder what my mom will eat while we're gone.

Which brings us full circle. I am back to worrying about my mother. It's a death grip, the worry. Even though I called Regina and gave her my cell phone number. Even though she promised to call me if anything bad happened. Still.

I will not think about her on this trip.

I will not think about her on this trip.

I will not think about her on this trip.

"*Stars,*" Marnie reads aloud from her magazine, "*they're just like us . . .* Okay. Are you ready for this, Anna?"

"Yeah."

"Are you sure? Because this is going to blow you away."

"I'm sure."

"Okay . . ." She pauses dramatically. "*Sofía Vergara eats bananas.*"

"Wow."

"I know," Marnie says.

"She eats *bananas*?"

"Yes, Anna, she does."

"Just like *me*?"

"Just like you. Look . . . there's even a picture."

"Well, I am stunned."

"I knew you would be. This is some fine journalism."

"I think we should keep reading."

"Yes," Marnie says. "I think we should."

I can feel my lips twitching. It's been so long since I smiled, my muscles are rusted. I'm like the Tin Man from *The Wizard of Oz*. Oilcan! Oilcan!

*   *   *

When we get to baggage claim, the sorority sisters are waiting. They see Marnie and scream:

Triiii DELTA! DELTA! DELTA DELTA DELTA!
Delta three, Delta tri,
I will be one till I die.
We're the best,
Sisters true,
We're Tri Delta, through and through!

You would think they'd be too old for this behavior. But no. They are so loud everyone in the airport is staring. The Sisters don't care. They come running over, pile on top of Marnie.

Harper, Scarlett, Caro, and Presley. Those are their names. I know because they were all in the wedding. Harper was Marnie's maid of honor and the rest were bridesmaids. Hard to forget, those four. Not just for their orange dresses, but for their dance moves and the gallons of champagne they drank at the reception.

"Anna!" Harper shrieks and hugs me. "Welcome to Hotlanta!"

"Thanks," I say, but my voice is drowned out. They are cheering again:

D with an E with an L,
L with a T with an A,
T with an R, R with an I,
Delta Delta Delta Tri!

Soon a security guard appears. He is straight out of a movie. Tall. Dark, wavy hair. *Bob Ferrari*, his name tag reads, like the sports car.

"Is everything okay here?" he asks, smiling at Marnie. She is the prettiest one, no contest. Even in sweatpants.

Marnie smiles, nods.

"Your friends are very loud."

"Oh," Caro, the little redhead, says in an exaggerated whisper. "Is this a library? We didn't realize." She is the sassy one. I remember from the wedding.

Bob Ferrari ignores her. To Marnie he says, "You look familiar."

"Do I?"

"Have we met?"

"I don't think so."

"Are you a model?"

"No."

"You should be. You're beautiful."

I expect Marnie to get flustered, but she doesn't. She almost seems to be enjoying herself. "You're sweet."

"What's your name?"

"Marnie."

"That's a beautiful name."

"Thank you."

"A beautiful name for a beautiful girl."

Someone get this guy a thesaurus!

Harper doesn't seem to appreciate the conversation either because she cuts it off. "Let me ask you something, Bob Ferrari," she says, throwing an arm around him. "Are you fast?"

"Yeah. Real original."

The rest of them jump in. "Are you faster than Bob Corvette?"

"And Bob Porsche?"

"And Bob Jaguar?"

They are cracking themselves up, but Bob isn't paying them any attention. He only has eyes for Marnie.

"We're sorry, Bob," Harper says finally. "We can't help ourselves. You see, we're reunioning."

"Reunioning?"

"I haven't seen them since November," Marnie explains.

"Oh yeah?"

"Yeah," Scarlett says. "She flew all the way from Rhode Island to see us, Bob."

"We just can't contain our excitement," Presley says.

"We played hooky from work, Bob," Caro whispers. "Shhhhh, don't tell my boss."

"Well, if you need anything while you're in town . . ." Bob reaches into his chest pocket and pulls out a business card. He hands it to Marnie and smiles just for her. Cleft chin and everything. "Call me."

For a second Marnie hesitates, holding the card. It occurs to me that this is a Charlie-and-the-Golden-Ticket moment, and most women would take it. And if Marnie were not married to my father and I were not standing here, this might be a different story.

But she is.

And I am.

"I can't," Marnie says, handing the card back to Bob. "I'm married."

"Really?"

"Really." She holds up her ring finger for proof.

"She has a baby, too," Scarlett says.

"And a stepdaughter," I feel free to add.

Bob notices me for the first time. "You're the step-daughter?"

I nod, because my face is suddenly burning and I don't trust my voice.

"Too bad," he says to Marnie.

"Well," Harper says, snatching the card right out of his hand, "*I'm* not married!"

And everyone laughs. Because Harper is so bold. And so funny. And she is also, in Marnie's words, "chronically single." Everyone else brought dates to the wedding. Scarlett brought Ford. Caro brought Trey. Presley brought Jason. Harper—even though she caught the bouquet when Marnie threw it and is therefore supposed to be getting married next—still has no one. Marnie says that Harper "intimidates men" because she is such a "strong, independent woman." She is as tall as a professional basketball player, with hair even curlier than mine, and a nose too big for her face.

I think Harper is an Amazon goddess, but Bob clearly doesn't see her that way.

I am a little surprised that he lets her keep his card. Then I remember something Dani told me once: *When the lights go out, boys don't care what you look like.*

I hope that's not true.

I hope that Bob gives Harper a real chance. I hope that when she calls him up and asks him out he says yes.

And I hope that—after spending time with her—he falls in love not just with her personality, but also with her height, and her crazy curls, and her big nose.

On second thought, a guy who can't come up with any adjectives other than *beautiful* probably doesn't deserve Harper. She is too smart for him.

* * *

Zooming down the freeway in Scarlett's SUV, it hits me that I am really in Atlanta, Georgia. I have never been anywhere, unless you count Boston—which I don't because it's practically my backyard—or Tenafly, New Jersey, where I only went to visit my grandma Collette in her nursing home. And it's not like I saw the New Jersey sights or anything. I just sat around playing backgammon and breathing in the smell of adult diapers and creamed corn.

Now I am seeing some sights.

"You see that sign?" Caro says. She is sitting next to me in the third row, pointing out the window. "The panda?"

"Yeah."

"We're only like a mile from Zoo Atlanta . . . And those lights over there? . . . Turner Field. Home of the Atlanta Braves."

"Cool," I say.

"Too bad they're not playing tonight. We could go to a game."

"What *do* you girls want to do tonight?" Presley asks. She is sitting in the second row, her feet in Marnie's lap.

"I don't know, sleep?" Marnie turns to me. "Right, Anna? No Jane to wake us up?" Without makeup, the circles under her eyes really stand out. I probably have them, too.

"Yeah," I say.

"Unacceptable!" Harper calls from the front seat. "There will be no sleeping on this visit!"

"No sleeping!" Scarlett echoes. "We're playing hooky for you!"

"*You* try having a baby," Marnie says.

"A *baby*?" Harper says. "I can barely take care of myself!"

"You got that right," Scarlett says.

There is a scuffle in the front seat.

"Hey! No smacking the driver!"

"How *is* that sweet baby of yours?" Presley asks Marnie.

"Amazing."

"I'll bet. Those pictures you posted . . . I just want to eat her."

"She is pretty scrumptious."

"Those *cheeks*," Caro says.

"I know. David calls her his little meatball."

"Awww."

"Shit!" Marnie suddenly jumps in her seat.

We all turn to look at her.

"What's wrong?" Caro says.

"I'm leaking!"

"What do you mean *leaking*?"

"Milk, okay? I'm breast-feeding. If I were home I would have fed Jane hours ago."

"Ohhhh."

"I need to pump. Now."

"Pull over!" Presley says to Scarlett.

"I can't pull over. We're on the freeway."

"Well, exit then. Something."

"Shit!" There is a new level of panic to Marnie's voice as she rustles around the bags at her feet. "Anna. Did you grab that black briefcase thingy?"

"What black briefcase thingy?"

"By the mudroom door, when we were leaving the house?"

"No."

"Are you sure?"

"Yes." I'm sure because I have no idea what she's talking about.

"Oh, God," Marnie moans.

"What?"

"That was my breast pump."

Ah.

"I knew I needed it. I put it right by the door . . ." Marnie's voice is taking on a hysterical edge. "But I was in such a rush to leave . . . God, I'm such an idiot! Look at me!"

We look. Her sweatshirt is soaked.

"I hate when that happens," Harper deadpans.

"I'm a milk cow!"

"I'm getting off here." Scarlett jerks the steering wheel, shooting us into the exit lane. "Just tell me what to do."

"Well, you could *not* kill us," Harper says. "There's a suggestion."

"Tell me where to *go*. Damnit, Prius, move!" This Scarlett yells at the car in front of us.

"Babies 'R' Us," Marnie says.

"Do we have a Babies 'R' Us?"

"I'm on it," Caro says, tapping away on her phone.

Harper reaches over and blasts Scarlett's horn. "This is a milk emergency, people! A MILK EMERGENCY!"

"Got it!" Caro says. She calls out the name of some highway.

"Could you please stop saying that word?" Presley shouts.

"What word? Highway?"

140

"Milk!"

"What's wrong with milk?" Marnie says.

"It's disgusting!"

"Milk is not *disgusting*. It's natural."

"Milk, it does a body good," Harper adds.

"Agh!" Presley cries. "I'm lactose intolerant! How do you guys always forget that?"

Everyone is laughing now, even Marnie.

"I miss you guys," she says.

"Of course you do," Harper says.

She and Marnie exchange a smile.

My stomach pangs, just for a second. *Dani*, I think. But then I snap out of it. I am in Atlanta, Georgia. I am on an adventure with a bunch of wild bridesmaids, and Dani is stuck in school with Mr. Pfaff, freewriting.

*　　*　　*

Half an hour later, we are at Harper, Scarlett, Caro, and Presley's apartment. It is in Westside, which, Harper tells us, is the only place to be. There are just two bedrooms, so they have to double up, but there are loft beds, and beanbag chairs, and cool posters everywhere. Marilyn Monroe. David Beckham with his shirt off. The Periodic Table of Mixology. There is one really messy bathroom, a kitchen with gold counters, an ant-sized patio, and a living room with a bar and a pool table, where Marnie is now sitting, pumping away with her brand-new pump.

Everyone but Presley is watching. You would think Marnie would be embarrassed, but no. You would think I would be embarrassed, watching my stepmother milk herself, but it happens to be pretty cool. Tubes and suction cups and this strange whoosh, whoosh, whooshing sound.

"Wow," Harper says softly.

Marnie nods. "I know. When I first started nursing I was afraid I wouldn't make enough."

"No problem now," Scarlett says.

"Nope," Marnie says. "I'm a regular milk dispenser."

And we all just keep staring.

After Marnie has filled two bottles, she lies back on the pool table, closes her eyes, and smiles.

"Better?" Caro says.

"I'm a whole new woman."

CHAPTER

14

PICTURE THIS, my first night in Atlanta: I am out to dinner with five overgrown sorority girls and we are all dressed identically. It is a replay of the wedding, only this time Marnie isn't the bride, and instead of matching bridesmaid dresses it's matching orange tank tops bedazzled with tiger paws. No joke.

I got one for you, too, Anna, Presley said back at the apartment when everyone was getting ready. *This will look so cute on you! You can be our mascot!*

Presley is their spirit leader. I remember this from the rehearsal dinner, when she led the entire wedding party in a song she wrote herself, all about my dad and Marnie.

"To Marnie!" she says now, raising her beer.

Harper, Caro, and Scarlett raise their beers and clink. "To Marnie!"

Marnie and I are drinking iced tea, which here they call "sweet tea." It is basically liquid sugar.

"And to Anna," Presley says, lifting her bottle higher. "Our future Clemson tiger."

"To Anna!"

Marnie meets my eye and smiles. "You're in for quite a night," she says.

I smile back. I am bedazzled with tiger paws, and I have butterflies in my stomach. But they're the good kind of butterflies, the giddy kind. My mother is a thousand miles away. Dani is a thousand miles away. School is a thousand miles away. The place we're eating, according to Harper, is very famous. On days of Georgia Tech football games, it serves more than thirty thousand customers. On just a regular day, it cooks two miles of hot dogs.

Right after we order, the front pocket of my jeans starts buzzing. My chest tightens for a moment, but when I pull out my phone, I see it's not Regina. It's Sarabeth Mueller.

whr wr u 2day? r u sick???

It is my first text ever, but nobody here knows that. Harper, Scarlett, Caro, and Presley give me way too much credit.

"Who's texting you? Is it a boy?"

"What's his name?"

"Is he cute?"

"Is he asking you out?"

"No," I tell them. "It is not a boy."

It is the perfect time to excuse myself. When I ask for the ladies' room, Harper points across the restaurant. Harper is their captain. She has planned this whole night. She knows where everything is.

Being a texting novice, I am now in a bathroom stall, painstakingly plunking out one letter at a time.

I-a-m-f-i-n-e-

Before I can finish, my phone rings.

"Hello?" I say.

"Hey. It's Sarabeth. I just texted you."

"I know. I was just texting you back."

"Are you okay?" she says.

"Yeah. I'm in Atlanta."

"Really?"

"Really."

"Why?"

I feel weird telling her about the broken glass, so I don't. I say this was a spontaneous adventure. Just me and my stepmother.

"That's so cool."

I can't help smiling. It *is* cool.

Silence for a moment, and I think maybe we have run out of things to talk about, but then she says, "So . . . talent show posters went up today . . ."

"Yeah?"

"November fourth. That gives us a month. I think we should do an act."

"What kind of act?"

If she says Irish step, there is no way I'm saying yes. I will tell her I have stage fright, which is not far from the truth. Thanks for asking, I will say, but no thanks. *Oh, and, Sarabeth? You may not want to Irish step by yourself either. Everyone makes fun of you when you do.* Of course, I will say this as nicely as possible, so I don't hurt her feelings.

"Singing," she says.

"Singing?"

"You, me, and Shawna. Like at my party. But a cappella."

"No instruments?"

"You heard Shawna's voice."

"Yeah," I say, "but that was your *basement*. I don't exactly see Shawna Wendall getting up onstage in front of the whole school."

"She's in."

"What?"

"Reese and Chloe and Nicole said no, but Shawna's in. She's fired up."

"Seriously?" I say.

Sarabeth laughs. "Seriously . . . So what do you think?"

I hesitate, picturing Dani and Jessa Bell and Whitney Anderson—and all those ninth-grade boys in the front row—laughing. I hate them for thinking they're better than everyone. I hate myself for caring.

"I know you love to sing, Anna."

"How do you know that?"

"Chorus elective. Fifth grade. You sang 'Corner of the Sky' from *Pippin*."

"You remember that?"

"Of course. You were good."

It's crazy, but I feel somewhat brave in this bathroom stall in Atlanta, Georgia, wearing my bedazzled tiger-paw tank top. "Okay."

"You'll do it?"

"I'll do it."

"Great," Sarabeth says. "So we'll talk about it when you get back?"

"Yeah."

"When's that going to be?"

"Wednesday."

"Cool. We'll talk Wednesday."

After I hang up, I walk back to the table, where the Sisters have been hitting the curly fries and beer at an impressive rate and the volume of their voices has increased fifty decibels since I left.

They are remember-when-ing. *Remember when we had that scavenger hunt with Theta Chi? Remember when we toilet-papered the Alpha Delta Phi house? Remember when Marnie ran naked through the quad?* At one point, Marnie laughs so hard iced tea shoots out her nose.

This is what she meant when I heard her on the phone saying, "I used to be fun." Marnie was the fun one. The one who stole the red velvet rope from the movie theater to win the scavenger hunt. The one who climbed the tree to paint three orange triangles on the roof of Alpha Delta Phi. The one who streaked through the quad. The way they describe Marnie, she sounds like the disco ball at every party. Not unlike my mother, I realize. If she and Marnie had gone to college together, they might have been friends for a while. The irony isn't lost on me. The line between "fun" and "crazy" is hard for most people to see. But I am not most people.

"See why we call your dad the *tiger tamer*, Anna?" Harper says. "See why we gave him that hat at the wedding?"

They did. They gave him a silky black top hat. Also

a press-on mustache. They gave him a whip, too, but that didn't come out until the reception.

"Hey," Marnie says. Her cheeks are rosy and her eyes are bright. "I have *not* been tamed."

She is smiling, but there is a little edge to her words. I'm not sure if anyone else catches it. I look at Harper, and she is laughing; this is all in good fun. Marnie is her best friend.

Our server appears. He has beers balanced on one tray, chili dogs on another. "Hey, Jeremy," Marnie says, reading his name tag. "Do I look like a fun girl? Be honest . . ."

Marnie waits. Jeremy looks her over. He has yellow hair flopping in his eyes. He has a long, skinny neck like Ichabod Crane.

"Yes," he says. "Definitely."

"See?" Marnie says.

Like this is proof.

*   *   *

After dinner we go to a place called Mustang Sally's. Harper's plan was country line dancing, but Marnie has other ideas. She wants to ride a mechanical bull. The man working the door is huge and dressed in a western shirt, jeans, and beat-up cowboy boots. He tells us the bull is named Fu Man Chu, and no one has ever ridden him for more than six seconds.

"I will," Marnie says. She is so sure.

Later, she'll tell us that she felt the same confidence about natural childbirth. While she was pregnant she was positive she could deliver Jane without any pain medication, but as soon as the contractions hit—*bam!*—she was screaming for drugs.

Marnie on a mechanical bull is a total spaz and hilarious to watch. Her first attempt, she flies off almost immediately. Her next, she lasts two seconds. After that, she squeezes hard with her legs and even manages to let go with one arm. She makes the most ridiculous noises as she bucks, part cowgirl, part howler monkey, and I'm laughing so hard my throat hurts. I look at the Sisters and they are laughing, too, snapping pictures with their phones.

A small crowd has gathered. Marnie is loving it. You can tell from her face. For a moment I almost wish I were the one up there, yeehawing and bucking around, but then Marnie flies off the bull. Hard.

From the sawdusty floor, she says, "Ouch."

We all laugh.

"No, seriously. My neck."

"Oh," Harper says. "Shit."

*   *   *

At midnight we are in the ER waiting for Marnie to see a doctor. Harper, Caro, Scarlett, and Presley are line dancing in the triage room, which is not exactly big enough to hold their dance moves. I try to keep up, but I can't, so I go over and stand by Marnie, who is talking to the nurse on duty.

"How did you hurt your neck?"

Marnie smiles, kind of. It is more of a grimace. "Riding a mechanical bull . . . it was stupid."

"Well," the nurse says, "it wasn't smart." She has lank, colorless hair and a smushed-in face. I'll bet if Marnie weren't so annoyingly beautiful, she would use a nicer tone.

"She was awesome!" Presley calls out, doing a kick and a spin. "She stayed on for, like, four seconds!"

The nurse ignores Presley. "Scale of one to ten. How much pain are you in right now?"

"I don't know," Marnie says. "An eight?"

"Wait here," the nurse orders. She huffs her way past Harper, Scarlett, Caro, and Presley, then huffs back a minute later. "Come with me," she says to Marnie. Then, to the line dancers, "This is a *hospital*, not a bar. Go wait in the *waiting room*."

"Sorry," Harper says. "We'll be good."

"Sorry, you guys," Marnie whispers on her way out the door. She tries to turn her head to blow us a kiss, then grabs her neck and cries, "Ouch!"

The Sisters head out into the waiting room, where there are at least a dozen people waiting. A dozen people staring at us in our bedazzled tiger-paw tank tops. It is completely mortifying. Also, kind of thrilling.

*　　*　　*

We don't get back to Westside until after two a.m. Marnie has been given a neck brace, a muscle relaxant, and two kinds of painkillers. Harper sets her up on the pull-out couch with a bunch of blankets and a heating pad. As soon as Marnie lies down, she calls my dad. As soon as she hangs up, the pills knock her out.

I lie awake on a blow-up mattress under the pool table, recapping the night. *That was fun*, I think. And, yes, crazy. But not in a defective brain chemistry kind of way. More in a wild night out with your girlfriends kind of way. Normal crazy, not sick crazy. I think about our outfits. I think about Marnie snorting sweet tea out her nose. I think about Jeremy the Waiter, and Fu Man Chu, and Nurse Sourpuss, and the Sisters line dancing through the emergency room at midnight.

Eventually I fall asleep to the sound of Marnie snoring.

Sometime later, I wake up to the sound of my own whimpering. The image in my head is so real it can't possibly be a dream. My mother is dead; I am sure of it. She is lying on the sawdusty floor, eyes bulging, face blue.

I pinch my thigh hard. Twice. Three times.

No. I am not at Mustang Sally's, looking down at my mother's broken neck. I am on an AeroBed in Westside Atlanta. I can hear Marnie's snores, coming from the pullout couch.

I think about waking her up, saying, *I had a bad dream*.

And Marnie would say, *Tell me*.

But as I catch my breath I realize how stupid I am being. My mother isn't *dead*. I know, because if she were, Regina would call my cell phone. She promised she would call if there was a problem, and she hasn't called. So everything is fine.

Go back to sleep, I tell myself. And somehow I do.

* * *

When I wake up again, sun is streaming through the window and Marnie is lying on the pullout couch, squinting at the ceiling.

"What time is it?" she groans.

"What time is it?" Harper releases the window shade and flops on top of Marnie. "It's ten o'clock, you sloths!"

"Ow!"

"Serves you right!" Harper says, steamrolling her. "We took off work for you. What do you think this is? College?"

"Ow!" Marnie cries again. "My neck!"

"It still hurts?" Harper sits up.

"Yes, it still hurts. I pinched a nerve. This was my one chance to sleep in and I couldn't even find a comfortable position."

"I'll get you some coffee," Harper says.

"I can't drink *coffee*. I'm nursing. My boobs are rocks right now."

"Tea? Cocoa? . . . Orange juice?"

"Juice would be nice." Marnie's voice softens. She reaches out one stiff arm to pat Harper's shoulder. "Thanks, Harp."

"You got it . . . Anna? Juice?"

"Sure," I say.

My throat is thick, my brain foggy. Last night's dream is still in my head, but I reassure myself that this is all it was: a dream. An arbitrary firing of brain cells— nothing more. Even though deep down I know that dreaming about my mother dying is not arbitrary.

I will not think about her today.
I will not think about her today.
I will not think about her today.

I sit up and follow Harper into the kitchen so Marnie can call my dad and pump in peace. I drink my juice and eat my cereal. I listen to Harper, Caro, Scarlett, and Presley argue about whose job is worse and which of them is the most justified in blowing off work to hang out with us. Event promotion assistant, food critic intern, middle-school drama teacher, or temp. My vote is for temp. Poor Scarlett. She has to answer phones for a construction company and she keeps hanging up on people and getting yelled at.

The whole time, I am not thinking about my mother. But then Scarlett says, "I would rather clean houses than answer phones." And, without any warning, a memory pops into my head. It is of my mom cleaning our whole kitchen—every crevice and nook and cranny—with Q-tips. She must have used five hundred Q-tips. I don't know how old I was, but I remember walking downstairs one morning and seeing her hunched over the counter, scrubbing away at one square inch of granite. I remember the strange, vague feeling that what I saw wasn't normal mother behavior.

Was she ever normal? I wonder. *When did the crazy kick in?* Then, of course, I start thinking about the dream again. I know that I will be thinking about it all day if I don't do something.

So I cave. I go out onto the patio and call Regina.

Regina answers in a good mood. She tells me that my mother ate breakfast this morning.

"She did?"

"Yup. Oatmeal and raisins." It may not sound like progress, Regina says, but this is the first solid food my mom has eaten since she got out of the hospital. Until now, all Regina could get her to swallow was a few sips of Ensure. "Baby steps, Anna. Baby steps."

"What is she doing now?" I ask.

"Sleeping."

"How do you know?"

"I'm right here in the living room with her, honey. I can see her chest rise and fall. She's fine."

I consider telling Regina about my dream, but decide that it is something I will keep to myself. Instead I tell her about our big day ahead. Harper planned the whole thing. We will drive to Stone Mountain—"the largest exposed piece of granite in the world"—and ride the cable car. We will visit Martin Luther King Jr.'s gravesite. We will drive around Midtown and see all the sights— the historic neighborhoods and Piedmont Park. Even though it's completely touristy, we will visit the World of Coca-Cola and have lunch at Underground Atlanta. Finally, we will cap off our day at the Peachtree Center for some shopping and dinner at the Sun Dial.

"Whoa," Regina says. "Fun."

"Yeah."

Through the sliding glass door I see Marnie shuffle into the kitchen in her neck brace, with her two bottles of milk. She very stiffly puts them in the refrigerator.

"I have to go," I tell Regina.

"Have a ball, honey," she says.

"I will."

"Don't worry about your mom. She's in good hands."

"Okay."

When I hang up, I picture Regina cupping her big, strong palms together, holding the most fragile egg.

CHAPTER
15

TWENTY-FOUR HOURS LATER, we are back on the plane. Marnie is quiet. I am looking at the hundreds of pictures I took with my phone. The Sisters, hamming it up on a cable car. Harper, sucking ice cream out the bottom of a cone. Presley, carrying Scarlett on her shoulders. Caro, hanging upside down from a Coca-Cola sign. Marnie, doing the robot in her neck brace.

My favorites are the ones from the Sun Dial. Last night, we got all dressed up and ate dinner 723 feet above the city. We had a 360-degree panoramic view of the Atlanta skyline. It was surreal. It felt like I was eating shrimp cocktail on another planet. I was older up there, more sophisticated. I used three different forks and drank virgin piña coladas.

I thought I would feel like a tagalong on this trip, but

I didn't. They made me feel like I was one of them. And unless Marnie tells me I can't, the next time she goes to Atlanta, I am going with her.

After I look at the pictures so many times they are burned on my brain, I put away my phone, sit back in my seat, and think, *Maybe I'll go to Clemson. Maybe I'll pledge Tri Delta. Maybe, after I graduate, I'll move to Westside Atlanta. Wouldn't that be the life? Eating breakfast every morning with your four best friends, laughing all the time, going out every night?*

And then Marnie ruins it. "I'm sorry, Anna," she says.

I hate when that happens. When the perfect bubble you've been blowing pops in your face.

"For what?" I say.

"For . . . all of this . . . I don't know what I was thinking."

"It was fun. Isn't that why we came?"

"It was—" She tries to look at me, but she can't turn her head. So she shifts her whole body in the seat. "This stupid neck brace. I feel like an idiot."

"Don't feel like an idiot."

"I do, though. I wanted this trip to be different."

I think about when we got back to the apartment last night. I assumed the Sisters would stay up all night, reminiscing and painting each other's nails. Instead, they went straight for pajamas.

"Wait," Marnie protested. "It's our last night together. Aren't we going to hang out?"

And Scarlett said, "I have to get up early. Work."

"Me too," Caro said.

Scarlett said she had to get up early and quit her temp job. "You'll just have to come visit again, Marn," she said. "Or move back."

There was a flurry of hugs and kisses and *It was so great to see you*'s, until it was just me and Marnie in the living room and Harper standing in the doorway, wearing a blue baby-doll nightgown that made her look even taller than usual.

"You guys need anything?" Harper asked.

"I don't think so," Marnie said. She was just sitting on the pullout couch in her Clemson sweatpants, pumping. She had a funny expression on her face—the kind where you're trying really hard to look cheerful but your eyes give you away.

Which is how she looks now.

"I want to be a good role model," she says. "For you."

"You are," I say. And she is. I hate to admit it, but she is. The whole time Harper, Scarlett, Caro, and Presley were drinking beer, Marnie drank iced tea. She wouldn't let Harper drive. She said no to cigarettes. She called my dad so he wouldn't worry.

Marnie tries to shake her head, but she can't. "Fighting with your father in front of you . . . it wasn't fair."

For a second I don't even know what she's talking about. Then I remember the towels. *You call that fighting?* I think. *You should have seen him and my mother.*

"Leaving Jane, dragging you here . . . I don't know what I was thinking. I'm still . . . figuring things out. How to be married. How to be a mom. How to not . . . erase myself in the process. Does that make any sense?"

"Kind of," I say.

"I needed . . ." Marnie sighs deeply. "I guess I just needed to check in with the old me. To make sure she was still there."

"Is she?"

"I think so. It's just . . . weird . . . I thought we would all move on to the next phase together. We'd have our crappy entry-level jobs and our wild nights out and then we'd all fall in love, and be in each other's weddings, and have babies together, you know? I never thought I'd be doing it alone."

"You're not alone."

"I know. It just feels that way." Marnie fiddles with her necklace. "I had all these friends, you know? In the Tri Delt house? And then half of us moved to Atlanta together, which was great, because it was basically an extension of college. But then, suddenly I meet your dad and I'm pregnant and I'm moving to Rhode Island. And now I have this baby, who I absolutely love, but I'm home with her every day and we're not exactly having stimulating conversations. And the other moms I've met . . ." Her voice trails off.

"What?"

"They're just . . . I don't know . . . older. They already have their little groups. When I took Jane to story hour? At the library? None of the other moms even *talked* to me. They just looked me up and down and went back to their conversations. You know? Like I wasn't good enough."

"They're jealous."

"What?"

"They're jealous. Because you're so pretty."

Marnie waves a hand in the air like I'm being ridiculous.

"It's true," I say.

I remember the first time I saw her. How mad I was. How I wished, for my mom's sake, that Marnie were plain-looking, even ugly. Dad's ugly new girlfriend. But wouldn't that have been worse, in a way? Even more ego crushing for my mom? Marnie couldn't win, I guess. She was doomed to be hated either way. And now I feel kind of bad. All year I have given her the cold shoulder. If I were a mom at library story hour, I would have ignored her, too. It never occurred to me that she might be lonely. She has my dad and Jane. The perfect little family. What more could she need?

"So, what . . ." I say. "Do you wish you still had your crappy entry-level job? And your wild nights out?"

"Sometimes," she says softly.

"You could go back to work," I suggest. And then, almost as an afterthought, "You and my dad could go out for a wild night and I could babysit."

"Thanks, Anna." Marnie smiles a little. Then, "I really do love him, you know."

"I know."

"When I met him . . . we met in the first month of my first real job. My first sales conference. I know this sounds stupid, but I was really excited about that conference. I guess I wish . . . if that had been my hundredth conference, if I had been thirty-three instead of twenty-three . . . But you can't choose when you fall in love. It just happens, you know?"

"Yeah," I say. Like I've ever been in love.

"Remember Harper's toast? At the rehearsal dinner?"

I nod.

Harper gave this funny speech comparing people to bagels and describing the kinds of bagels she could and could not be friends with. Pumpernickel: there for you in an emergency. Marble: two-faced. French toast: overly sweet. Onion: nice to hang out with occasionally, but sticks around too long and can't take a hint. The everything bagel, Harper told us, was the noblest bagel. The all-of-the-above friend, the partner for life.

"I remember," I say.

I also remember how I felt when Harper said that Marnie and my dad were everything bagels. Pissed. If anyone was an everything bagel, my *mom* was an everything bagel. *She* was the partner for life.

"Right," Marnie says. "That's what Harper told everyone. That your dad and I were made for each other. But then she drank a bunch of margaritas and cornered me in the bathroom and told me she thought I should wait. I shouldn't marry him yet. I was too young. Anna, do you know what I did? I got mad. I accused her of being jealous. Of not wanting me to be happy. We had this big fight, the night before my wedding. And you know what, she was right! I *was* too young. Sometimes I feel like I'm . . . just . . . I don't know . . . *playing house*. But the thing is, I love your dad. And Jane and you. And I feel so lucky. And I'm really sorry I dragged you into my drama."

"You didn't."

"Yes, I did. I've been an emotional roller coaster lately."

Emotional roller coaster? Really? If my mother is the

Goliath ride at Six Flags, with 194-foot drops and 102-foot reverse loops, Marnie is the kiddie coaster.

"I think it's the hormones."

"No offense," I say, "but you've got nothing on my mom."

"Oh, Anna. I didn't mean—"

"I know," I say, cutting her off. "Just . . . I'm glad we came."

"You are?"

"Yeah. I had fun."

Silence for a moment.

Then, apropos of nothing, I say, "Bob Ferrari."

And Marnie laughs, like I knew she would.

*　　*　　*

My father and Jane are waiting in baggage claim. Marnie runs—literally runs, neck brace and all—to meet them. She unstraps Jane from the BabyBjörn, hugs her, leans into my dad, and bursts into tears.

"Hey," my father says gently. "Hey, bucking bronco."

Is it my imagination, or are his eyes shiny, too? Sheesh. Talk about drama.

"Hi, Anna," he says. He puts an awkward arm around my shoulders. This is how we do the hug thing.

"Hi, Dad."

Marnie is now ripping off her neck brace and kissing Jane everywhere. Ear. Cheek. Belly. She's going to eat her, it looks like.

"How was the trip?" my father asks me.

"Good," I say.

"Good. That's good."

Marnie holds up one of Jane's feet. Polka-dot sock. She holds up the other one. Stripes.

"What can I tell you?" my father says. "We had a wild time. We made *sales calls*. We ate *organic rice cereal*."

Marnie smiles. They kiss, pull apart, then kiss again.

"Don't mind us," I say. I look at Jane, who's peering at me over Marnie's shoulder. "Your mom and dad are gross, huh?"

CHAPTER
16

AT LUNCH THE NEXT DAY, Sarabeth holds up one of the flyers that have been posted around school. *Got talent? SHMS Talent Show: Friday, November 4, 7:30 p.m.*

"We need a name for our act," Sarabeth says, and right away Nicole says, "The Moon Goddesses." Shawna snorts, but that doesn't stop Nicole and Chloe from coming up with a bunch of other gems. The Widdershins. Mortar and Pestle. Black Magic.

The rest of us exchange looks.

"We are not naming ourselves anything Wiccan related," Shawna says.

"Fine," Nicole says. "Why don't you come up with your own name, then? We're not even in your act."

"I am too stunned by those horrible suggestions to think."

"Hey now," Sarabeth says. "No fighting, no biting."

"Funny you should mention biting," Chloe says. "During the height of the witch trials, the witch's mark—or *devil's mark*, as some called it—actually looked like a bite mark."

"Cool," Sarabeth says.

Reese points to the jersey she's wearing. "Why not the Longhorns?"

"Um," Nicole says, "because they're not football players from Texas?"

Reese shrugs. "They're not witches either."

Shawna snickers.

"We're whatever we decide to be," Sarabeth says. "We just need a name."

*　　*　　*

In gym class, Chloe and I have a field day.

"I think you should be the Sweaty Socks," she says. "You can dress up like eighth-grade boys."

"Or Athlete's Foot," I say. "We can sing into cans of Lotrimin."

"No, I've got it," Chloe says. "The Jock Straps."

*　　*　　*

"Here's a name," Reese says to me as we're walking out of social studies. "Bacon's Rebellion."

"The Puritans," I say.

"The Fundamental Orders of Connecticut."

"The Patroons."

"Crap," Reese says. "I forget what patroons are . . . Is that going to be on the test?"

"Owners of large estates."

"Oh, right."

*　　*　　*

"It's obvious who we have to be," Shawna says in study hall.

"Is it?"

"Yes."

"This should be good."

She waggles her silvery black fingernails in the air. *"Gobsmacked."*

I look at her blankly.

"Best color ever."

"I know, but what does it mean?"

"Completely shocked, astounded, flabbergasted, speechless with amazement." Shawna reaches out, gives my cheek a little slap. "To be struck dumb as if by a smack in the face."

I give her a little slap back.

She laughs. "Exactly. That's how people are going to feel when they hear us sing."

*   *   *

Later, Shawna and I are walking to the buses together.

"Gobsmacked," I say. "It has a nice ring to it."

"Onomatopoeia. It sounds the way it feels."

"Are you speaking from experience?"

"Sure," Shawna says. "I've been gobsmacked. Everyone has. It's part of the human condition."

This is when I hear it. "Anna! Anna Banana!" A disembodied voice, coming from the parking lot. "Yoo-hoo!"

It is unmistakable.

"Oh, God," I murmur.

Shawna looks at me curiously.

"I'll see you tomorrow." I don't even try to explain. I just hightail it over to Regina's car. She's got the window rolled down and one big plaid flannel arm waving.

"Surprise!" Regina's voice is so loud the whole bus line can hear.

"Hey," I say quietly. "What are you—"

"Anna."

I look at the passenger seat and there is my mother.

My hand flies to my mouth.

"Hi," a voice says behind me.

I turn around and there is Shawna.

"Shawna Wendall," she says, reaching out a hand for Regina to shake. "I'm a friend of Anna's."

"Regina Rose," Regina booms. "I'm a friend of the family."

"Shawna Wendall," Shawna repeats, reaching her arm through the window for my mother to shake.

"Frances Collette," my mother says softly. "Anna's mom."

I give Shawna a look, but she either doesn't see it or deliberately ignores it. Her eyes flit from my mom to me and back to my mom. "Wow. You two look so much alike."

There is no way Shawna means this. Seeing my mom after three weeks is kind of horrifying. Her hair is limp around her face. Her skin is pasty. There are bags under her eyes and wrinkles around her mouth I've never seen before. She looks old. When I walk around the car to hug her, I smell cigarettes.

"I wanted to surprise you." Her voice is low and gravelly. "I missed you."

My mother is here. She's not dead. I should be happy, but all I can think is, *Who is this person?*

"I missed you, too," I murmur.

Shawna makes herself at home, leaning against the car. "Were you on a trip, Mrs. Collette?"

My mother shakes her head. "I've been in the hospital. I had a very bad bout of depression."

Shawna stares at her and then nods. "I'm sorry to hear that."

"Thank you for being here for Anna."

"T's okay."

I can't believe what I'm hearing. I want to jackhammer a hole in the parking lot and dive in.

I don't know how it happens, but Shawna ends up in Regina's car, getting a ride home. It's quiet in the car and I can feel her glancing at me. I can't look at her, but out of the corner of my eye I see her take out a piece of paper and write something down. Before she gets out of the car, she hands it to me.

555-6602.

*   *   *

After we drop Shawna off, my mother climbs into the backseat with me.

"Hi," she says, and starts putting on her seat belt. Which is a good sign, I guess. She doesn't want to die in a car crash.

"Hi," I say.

"It's nice to see you."

"It's nice to see you, too." *Nice* is such a beige word. A nothing word.

She doesn't say anything else, just sits there. A different kind of mother might scoot over, wrap her arms around me. But she has never been like that. Keesha Soboleski's mom was the kissy-huggy type and I always thought it was weird how as soon as Keesha got off the bus they would run into each other's arms like lovers after a long war. If my mom ever did that, I would die from shock. But still. She could at least look at me.

Regina drives us around, playing music on the radio, stopping at the drive-thru for sodas, like she is the chauffeur and my mother and I are on a date. I know Regina is dying for us to talk, to fill in the hole of the last three weeks. But the hole is too big. There is too much that needs to be said to fill it, and so we say nothing.

At some point, Regina stops for gas, getting out of the car to pay and leaving us alone.

"How's Dani?" my mother asks.

I stare at her. There is no way she has forgotten this. She was *there* that day when I got home from Brickley's Ice Cream. She gave me a whole speech about female socialization. She busted out the book *Queen Bees and Wannabes* and read me a passage out loud.

"We're not friends anymore, remember?"

"Oh, right."

She remembers nothing. That much is clear.

So I tell her again. I tell her about Dani, and when I'm done with that I keep going. I tell her about Sarabeth the Irish stepper and Shawna the eyebrow plucker. I tell her about Reese from Texas and the Wiccan twins and the talent show. I tell her about Mr. Pfaff's goatee and Ms. Baer-Leighton's sawed-off haircut. The words spill out of me, and it's weird because my mother doesn't interrupt once. In the past she would be putting in her two cents, telling me what she thinks. Offering advice. But this time she doesn't.

Maybe she is too tired to interrupt. Maybe she isn't even listening, but I keep talking. At some point, she does something totally out of character. She reaches across the seat and takes my hand. Her fingers are so cold. I hate how cold they are. It makes me feel like I am the mother and she is the little kid who forgot her mittens. And that's not how it's supposed to be.

But I hold her hand anyway. And by the time Regina pulls into my father's driveway, her fingers are warm.

"Thanks for the ride," I say.

"Anytime," Regina says.

When I let go of my mother's hand to pick up my backpack, she grabs it again. She squeezes harder. "I'm sorry," she says.

I feel my stomach clench. "It's okay, Mom."

"I'm so sorry."

"I know."

"No," she says, a little fiercely, as though I still haven't heard her. "I'm sorry, Anna. I need you to believe me."

"I do, Mom."

"I'll try to be better."

"Okay."

*　　*　　*

I walk into my father's house, feeling like crap. Why do I feel like crap? I think about the bags under my mother's eyes. The smell of cigarettes. The break in her voice when she said good-bye. What if she never gets well? What if I have to live here, in my father's house, until I graduate from high school?

I walk into the kitchen, but instead of Marnie and Jane waiting for me, there is my father sitting at the table, typing away on his laptop. His skin is tan. His shirt is crisp. His hair is gelled. And I don't know why, but the sight of him pisses me off.

"What are *you* doing here?" I say, throwing my backpack on the floor.

He looks up. "Well, hello to you, too."

"Where's Marnie?"

"Upstairs, taking a nap with Jane. How was school?"

"Stupid."

"Stupid, huh?" He closes the laptop, settles back in his chair. "What was stupid about it?"

"Why aren't you at work?"

"I worked from home today. Jane was up a lot last night and Marnie barely slept, so I wanted to help out."

"Huh," I say.

"Anyway, I'm finished working. It's Wednesday."

"So?"

"It's our night."

"I thought we were done with that."

"Done with Denny's?"

"I've been living here for the past three Wednesdays, and we haven't gone to Denny's once."

"Ah." My father nods. "Well, I wanted to give you time to get settled in and everything, spend some time with Marnie and Jane . . ."

"Right."

"Come on." He stands up. "We'll eat cheese fries. You can tell me how stupid school is."

"Dad."

"Or not. We don't have to talk about school. We can just eat cheese fries."

"I saw Mom."

"Right." My father clears his throat, drums on the table a few times. "I know. Regina called earlier."

"Were you not going to say anything? Were you not even going to ask how she is?"

"How is she?"

"You should have seen her." My voice wobbles. "She looked awful."

Silence.

"She was like a zombie."

"The medication your mother is taking, Anna," my father says, "antidepressants and mood stabilizers—they take time to reach full efficacy. It could be another week or two before there's a measurable change in her symptoms."

So matter-of-fact. So clinical. So *missing the point*.

I am sick of this. I am so sick of this, I can't even see straight. It is shame and embarrassment and loss and betrayal and sadness and anger all rolled up together. Why doesn't he get it?

"You bailed," I murmur.

"What?"

"You bailed on her. So many times."

"Anna—"

"No, Dad. You did. Whenever Mom got depressed, you suddenly had a *sales trip*." I scratch quote marks in the air. "What—you couldn't work from home *then*? Your *sales trips* were so important?"

My father shakes his head. "That's not fair."

I look at him, standing there in his starched white shirt, and I think, Marnie got the upgrade. My mom got the old version, but Marnie got Husband 2.0. Diaper changer. Kale eater. Worker from home.

"You're right," I say. "It wasn't fair."

He frowns.

"Why are you making that face?"

"I'm not making a face."

"You are," I say. "You always do when we're talking about Mom. Why do you hate her so much?"

"I have never said I hated her."

"No? Then why didn't you help her?"

"Anna—"

"Why did you check out every time she got sick? Huh, Dad? Why didn't you deal with it? Why did you call Regina every single time?"

"That's an exaggeration."

"Not to me."

"Regina's a nurse," he says.

"So?"

"So, she knew about depression."

"*You* know about depression. You sell drugs for a living!"

"She's your mother's best friend."

"*You* were her husband! And you left! You quit on her!"

My father shakes his head. "You know what? This is not a conversation we're going to have right now." He picks up a glass from the table and walks it over to the sink so he won't have to look at me.

I follow right behind him. "Then when are we going to have it?"

"Why don't you go do your homework? You must have a lot to catch up on."

"I don't care about homework."

"You should care about homework. School is important."

"*This* is important! I care about *this*!"

"Calm down, Anna."

"I'll calm down when you tell me why you left! And don't tell me marriage is complicated. And don't tell me it's no one's fault. Don't tell me any of that crap, just tell me the truth!"

He whips around to look at me. "I tried, okay? Don't you think I tried? I'm not the bad guy here!"

"So, what—you're blaming Mom?"

"I'm not *blaming* her. I'm just saying . . . your mother had a choice. She had medication for depression and she wouldn't stay on it. She didn't like how it made her feel. What was I supposed to do, jam it down her throat?"

"Maybe. Yeah."

We're staring at each other.

"She's an adult, Anna. She's in charge of her own bad decisions."

"*You're* an adult. You're in charge of *your* own bad decisions."

"Do you think I'm proud that I couldn't make my marriage work?"

"I don't know, *Dad.*" I really emphasize the word, and I know how awful it sounds because I see him wince. And that wince makes me want to cry. "Why didn't you take me with you?" I whisper. "Why didn't you even try to get custody?"

My father looks at me, stunned. "Is that what you wanted? For me to get custody?"

I shrug.

"Because . . . I'm confused . . . you wouldn't even stay over in my apartment."

"That was *after* you already decided. You never even asked me what I wanted. You just said, *Anna, we're getting a divorce. This is how it's going to be.*"

"We didn't want to drag you into it."

"You didn't want to *drag me into it*?"

"It was an adult decision."

"An *adult decision*?"

"Based on what the mediator suggested. Based on what we thought were your best interests at the time."

"My *best interests*?" I'm beginning to sound like a parrot.

"Yes. Your mother was your primary parent. She was home more. I traveled for work—"

"You think it was in *my best interests* to find her almost dead?"

"No." My father shakes his head and blows out a gust of breath. "No, absolutely not. I had no idea that was going to happen. If I had . . . if I could take it back . . . I'm sorry, Anna."

I nod. It's the first time he's apologized to me, and it's not clear if he's apologizing for his own actions or for my mom's. It doesn't matter, really. You can't take anything back.

"I'm going to bed," I say.

My father looks at his watch. "It's only four forty-five."

"I'm tired."

"What about dinner?"

"I'm not hungry."

He nods, reaching out a hand for an awkward shoulder pat, but I am already walking away.

Later, I hear him in the bedroom with Marnie. I know they're talking about me because I hear my name. In the past, I would have tried to eavesdrop, but now I don't even care what they're saying. When my father comes to check on me, I pretend I'm asleep.

CHAPTER
17

IN ENGLISH, Mr. Pfaff takes one look at me and tells me to go see the school counselor. I start to argue with him, but he says, "This is not a suggestion, Anna. This is an imperative." Sometimes I wonder if Mr. Pfaff sits around all weekend reading the dictionary. Is it part of his job description to use big words? Am I supposed to be impressed? Because I'm not.

Anyway, here I am in Mrs. Ramondetta's office, which is the last place I want to be. Although she is not remotely intimidating. In her crew-neck sweater and cargo pants, with her shiny brown hair in a ponytail, she looks more like a student than a school counselor. She also has a comfortable couch and an impressive assortment of lollipops, and she doesn't ask a lot of questions. She just lets me sit here, sucking on a root beer Dum Dum.

It feels like a long time. Long enough for me to suck the whole thing and start chewing on the stick.

"Would you like another?" Mrs. Ramondetta asks quietly, holding out the basket.

"No, thanks," I say.

More silence.

Then, "What's on your mind, Anna?"

I don't know how to answer that.

"I don't force anyone to talk," she says. "You can just sit here if you like."

So I do. I just sit here, chewing on my stick.

She has a lot of patience, Mrs. Ramondetta. I wonder how my mother does it. I can't picture her, sitting in her counseling office, waiting quietly for some messed-up kid to have a lightbulb moment. When she's not depressed, my mom loves to talk. She hates sitting still. She is motion and action and words and song. But I don't know what she's really like in there, Dr. Frances Collette, PhD. She had to be doing a decent job, right, over the years? She wasn't falling asleep at her desk or crying in front of students or flashing the principal or anything, because if she had been, they'd have fired her. Maybe, like Dani's uncle Patrick, an alcoholic who's always hiding his bottles in the toilet tank, my mother just got very good at hiding her crazy.

"How's your mom doing?" Mrs. Ramondetta says.

I hate when that happens. I hate when you're relaxing on the couch, thinking a private thought, and someone suddenly jumps right in and asks you about it, because—oh yeah—she knows all your personal business.

"She's fine," I say.

"Fine?"

"She's a school counselor, like you. How could she have any problems?"

It's a joke, and it's lame, which explains why Mrs. Ramondetta doesn't get it. "You think because someone has a master's degree in psychology she can't have any problems?"

"PhD," I say.

"Pardon?"

"My mom has a PhD in psychology, not a master's."

"Oh." Mrs. Ramondetta looks surprised. "Wow."

"She got it at Brown."

"That's quite a school. Ivy League."

"Yeah. Things are really working out for her." I help myself to another lollipop. Peach this time. I unwrap it, take a few sucks.

"Tell me more," Mrs. Ramondetta says.

"About?"

"About how things are working out for your mom."

"I was being sarcastic."

"Yeah. I caught your drift."

She caught my drift. She even *sounds* like a teenager. I wonder if my mother ever does that—tries to sound cool just to get kids to talk. It's a pretty flimsy technique if you ask me. More master's than PhD.

"She has bipolar two," I say.

"Oh?"

"Have you heard of it?"

"I have."

"The doctor she used to go to? Dr. Amman? He thought she was just depressed. But now, I guess, there's this whole other part to it. Mania, they call it."

Mrs. Ramondetta nods. She helps herself to a lollipop, and as she unwraps it I tell her what Regina told me. About how my mom's periods of "high" and "low" can be really short, with long stretches of "normal" in between, which explains why it took so long for her to get this new diagnosis.

"From what I've read," Mrs. Ramondetta says, "some people may not even realize they *have* a mood disorder, and it's only those closest to them who are affected."

"Oh, she has one all right," I say. "Believe me."

"I believe you."

"She's on mood stabilizers and everything."

"That's good. It sounds like your mom's on the right track."

I shrug, suck on my lollipop, glance around the room.

There's a plant on Mrs. Ramondetta's desk that could use some serious water. It's all brown and crispy.

"So who's your support system?"

"Hmm?"

"The people you talk to about your mom. The ones who get it." She has put her lollipop down on her armrest and is leaning forward, propping her elbows on her knees.

I shrug.

"Your dad?"

I snort.

"No?"

"They're divorced."

"And . . ."

"And my mom is not exactly his favorite subject."

"Okay . . . we can talk about that next time . . . What about grandparents?"

"I only have one grandmother. She's in a nursing home in New Jersey. I never see her."

"Are there other adults in your life? People you're close to?"

"Regina, I guess."

"Who's Regina?"

"My mom's best friend."

"And you can talk openly with Regina, about how you're feeling? How you're coping with your mom's depression?"

I shrug. "We don't really talk about me."

"What do you talk about?"

"My mom. What she's eating. How much she's sleeping."

"What about friends?" Mrs. Ramondetta says. "Which friends do you talk to about your mom?"

I stare at her. "I don't talk to my friends about my *mom*."

"Why not?"

"It's . . . I don't know . . . embarrassing."

"It's embarrassing that she has a chemical imbalance in her brain?"

I shake my head. That's not what I mean.

"Would it be embarrassing if she had cancer?"

"No."

Mrs. Ramondetta cocks her head at me, waiting.

"What—you think I should just tell people that my mother tried to *kill herself*? That she got put in the *mental ward*?"

"Why not?"

"Are you kidding me?"

"They're your mom's actions, not yours."

"Yeah, but she's my *mom*."

"That's right," Mrs. Ramondetta says. "She's your *mom*. One of the most important people in your life. Which means that you are intimately affected by what's happened. And you need some support."

Oh, God. This. *This* is the crap I was trying to avoid. I would have told her so much more if she hadn't suddenly made this about me. I am not the one with the problem. I am not my mother.

"Anna." Our eyes are completely level because Mrs. Ramondetta is leaning in and I am slouching back.

I focus on a piece of lint on her left shoulder.

"You can keep holding it in. You can keep trying to deal with everything on your own. But how's that working out for you? Think about it. Why are you here?"

By now, I have crunched the peach lollipop to shards and I am grinding the shards with my molars.

"It got me out of English," I say, giving a little shrug. "And free lollipops."

Mrs. Ramondetta smiles. There's a gap between her teeth. "Humor's a great coping mechanism, Anna. I'm glad you're using it."

It is so obvious what she's doing, the whole candy and positive feedback thing, trying to show that she is "on my side"—that she "understands what I'm going through." Too bad I can see right through it.

"I know what you're doing," I say.

"What am I doing?"

"You're trying to be my buddy."

"And that's wrong because . . ."

I shrug. There's nothing *wrong* with it. Mrs.

Ramondetta is being perfectly nice. Too nice, maybe. She reminds me a little of Marnie, actually, except instead of feeding me rice chips she's feeding me lollipops.

"It's okay to lean on people, Anna," she says. "It doesn't make you weak."

"I know that."

"It doesn't make you your mother either."

I look up, my eyes meet Mrs. Ramondetta's, and my throat aches a little. For a moment, I think I might cry. But I don't. I grab another lollipop, unwrap it and start sucking. Then the bell rings.

"I have study hall," I say.

"Come back and see me anytime, Anna," Mrs. Ramondetta says. "My door is always open."

*   *   *

After school, Marnie and Jane are baking something in the kitchen. I am in the den, watching Animal Planet, but instead of feeling happy about it, I'm bummed. There are only two people who love Animal Planet as much as I do: my mother and Dani. And they are not here. A part of me is tempted to call Dani's house. I pick up the phone. I even start dialing the number, but then I stop myself. I imagine her saying, *Why are you calling me, Anna? We're not friends anymore, remember?* She's probably not even home right now. She's probably off shaking her pom-poms or kissing Ethan Zane under the bleachers.

I call up Regina to see if she and my mom are watching. But the answer is no. My mother is taking a bath, Regina says. And Regina would rather stick pins under her fingernails than watch Animal Planet.

"The bath is a good sign," Regina says.

"Yeah," I say.

And I hang up, thinking I should feel better. But I don't.

I wonder if Sarabeth Mueller watches Animal Planet. I think about calling her, but then I remember she has Irish step on Thursdays.

So I find the scrap of paper with Shawna Wendall's number on it. I dial it and say, "This is Anna Collette."

And Shawna says, "About time you called. Whatcha doing?"

And I say, "Watching Animal Planet."

And she says, "What's on?"

And I say, "Sloths."

And she says, "I am all over that."

And somehow, we end up watching the whole thing together, from our separate couches.

"First of all," Shawna says when the show is over, "sloths are awesome."

"Agreed."

"Second, I would make an excellent sloth. I could sleep twenty hours a day, easy."

"So could my mother." I don't mean to say it. The words just slip out, and when they do, I panic. I try to think of something—anything—to cover it up.

"That's really common," Shawna says matter-of-factly. "Sleep changes are, like, the number one sign of depression. Right up there with feelings of helplessness and weight loss."

"How do you—"

Shawna cuts me off. "Amateur psychologist, remember?"

"Right."

"I read a lot of psych books."

"Oh." I hesitate. Then, "You're not going to, you know . . ."

"Tell anyone about your mom?"

"Yeah."

"Not if you don't want me to."

"I don't. I mean . . . I'm not ashamed or anything, I just . . . you know . . ."

"I know," Shawna says. "I get it."

I think she might be talking about her eyebrows, but I can't be sure. She doesn't say anything else, and I don't want to make her feel self-conscious by bringing up the subject. So I don't. I just say, "Thanks."

"No problem. It was fun slothing out with you."

"Ditto."

"In study hall tomorrow, we should work on getting our tongues to extend ten to twelve inches so we can pick up leaves."

"Sounds good," I say.

" 'Bye, sloth."

"See ya."

CHAPTER
18

ON FRIDAY NIGHT, Sarabeth drags me and Shawna to another football game. This one is away, against William Allen, the Quaker school in Providence. Mrs. Mueller drops us off at the same time the Shelby Horner cheerleaders are exiting the bus. Dani looks surprised to see me, but this time I just turn my head like I don't see her.

Sarabeth is in full Shelby Horner form, with stripes of blue and gold on her face. When we get to the bleachers, she offers to do mine, and I let her.

"We need to represent," she says, smearing paint on my cheeks. "William Allen is tough. Their quarterback threw twenty-eight touchdowns last season."

Shawna scoffs.

"I'm painting you next, Wendall," Sarabeth says.

"No you're not."

"I am. You best prepare yourself."

*   *   *

Everything is fine for the first half. We sit right next to the Shelby Horner band. "Band-Aids," Shawna calls us, because at one point we start air drumming and air tuba playing and air saxophoning right along with them. We know we are dorking out, but there is something about being at another school and being in a group and wearing face paint that makes it acceptable.

At halftime, we walk to the concession stand. There are William Allen kids everywhere. I see a group of boys eyeing us. They are all hair gel and Under Armour, older looking, somehow, than Ethan Zane and his group. One of them is looking at me and I can't help looking back. Why not? I think. He's cute. And I'm emboldened by the fact that I will never see him again after tonight.

But then something happens. There's a snort of laughter. A finger pointing at Shawna.

"Dude, check out those eyebrows."

"Holy shit, it's Morticia Addams!"

"Hey, Morticia. What are you doing at a football game? Shouldn't you be home with Uncle Fester?"

They're just about killing themselves laughing.

"Keep walking," Sarabeth murmurs. "Ignore them."

"Where ya goin', Morticia?"

"Back to the morgue?"

Now they're following us.

A rage builds up inside me. I don't know where it's coming from, but I'm turning around, facing them.

"Shut up."

The biggest one, with thick, dark hair and a smirk on his face, looks at his friends. "Did she just tell me to shut up?"

"Yes, I did, Mr. Hair Gel, Mr. I'm So Cool I Wear Under Armour So I Can Make Fun of Anyone Who's Not as Cool as Me. You go to a *Quaker school*. Isn't it against your religion to be a jackass?"

I'm yelling, and I know I'm making a scene, but I don't care.

For a second, the kid looks shocked. Then he mutters, "Freaks," and motions for his buddies to walk away.

I turn to Shawna and see tears in her eyes.

"No one's ever stuck up for me before," she says.

"That's what friends do," I say. And I don't know why, but there are tears in my eyes, too.

*   *   *

We miss the second half of the game. The three of us spend the next hour sitting on a patch of grass by the parking lot.

"Are you okay?" Sarabeth asks Shawna.

And Shawna tells Sarabeth what she's already told me, about her eyebrows. "That's why I transferred to Shelby Horner last year," she says quietly. "Kids made fun of me all the time. It got so bad I'd pretend to be sick so I didn't have to go to school."

"Kids can be so mean," Sarabeth says.

I know she is speaking from experience, but I don't expect her to start listing all the names she's been called. Casper the Ghost, Skim Milk, Albino, Powder, X-ray, Whitey Bulger.

I can't believe she's saying those things aloud. Turning her insides out. Am I supposed to remind her that I was Pubes in sixth grade? Because I won't. I hated being Pubes.

But here we are, huddled together on the grass. Shawna's on one side of me, Sarabeth is on the other, and our knees are touching and we're breathing in the same air, and something about it makes me feel safe.

"My mother's sick. She has bipolar depression and she tried to kill herself four weeks ago. She's out of the hospital, but I don't know if she's ever going to get better."

No one says anything. *Are you happy, Mrs. Ramondetta?*

Then I feel Shawna's hand on my shoulder. "That kid back there was right," she says. "We are a bunch of freaks."

Sarabeth jumps all over her. "Shawna! What kind of comment is that? Did you hear what Anna just said? You're supposed to be her friend!"

Shawna's looking at me and there's blue and gold paint smeared all over her face. I'm sort of half-laughing, half-crying, and I can feel the paint running down my face, too. I'm a mess, but strangely I don't care.

"Everyone's got their shit," Shawna says, "is all I meant. It was a statement of unity."

"Ha," I say.

Shawna clasps my knee. "I'm here for you, Anna."

Now Sarabeth is saying it, too. "I'm here for you, Anna. We both are." No one says I shouldn't worry. No one tells me my mother will be fine. No one offers stupid advice. They're just there.

Later, when Mrs. Mueller is driving us home and we're cleaning off our faces with tissues, Sarabeth says, "Maybe we should own it. The Freaks."

"What do you mean *own it*?" Shawna says.

"For our talent show act. Maybe that's what we should call ourselves."

"Actually," I say, glancing at Shawna, "I think we already have a name."

*   *   *

When I get back, my father and Marnie are in the den, watching a movie. "Hey, Anna," Marnie says when she sees me standing in the doorway.

"Hey."

"How was the game?"

"Good."

"Did you win?" my father says.

"Uh-huh." I don't actually know if we won. I spent the whole second half in the parking lot, pouring my guts out. But they don't need to know that.

"Want to join us?" Marnie says. "It's *The Amazing Spider-Man*."

"No, thanks."

I go into the kitchen to get myself a drink and, strangely, my father follows.

"Are you hungry?" he says as I open the fridge and take out a can of seltzer.

"No."

"I can make you something if you want. Peanut butter and jelly? . . . Eggs?"

"You gave me money for dinner, remember?"

"Right." He nods.

It's weird. I never got an allowance before. If I needed something, my parents would just buy it. But ever since

I started staying here, my dad has been giving me money. Ten bucks here. Twenty bucks there. Tonight he gave me thirty bucks for the football game, which was way more than I needed. It's like he's trying to make up for something. Which maybe he should be.

"What'd you have?" he says.

"What?" I pop open the can.

"To eat."

"Oh. A hot dog. And popcorn."

"That's not very much. You sure I can't make you something?"

"Yeah, Dad." I give him a funny look. "Since when do you care how much I eat?"

"I care."

"Whatever," I mutter, taking a sip of seltzer. I am done trying to have serious discussions with him. After my last attempt, I realize it's not worth it. We're better off keeping our conversations short and superficial.

"Enjoy the movie," I say, turning to go.

"Anna?"

"What."

"Can you hang out a minute? There are a few things I need to say to you."

I turn back around, take a slow sip of seltzer. Then another.

"Anna?"

"I'm listening."

"Okay . . . first, I'm glad you went to see the school counselor."

I stop drinking. *"What?"*

"I'm glad you went to see the school counselor."

"No, I heard you. I'm just . . . *seriously*? You talked to Mrs. Ramondetta?"

He shakes his head. "No. But I did speak with your principal yesterday, and—"

"You spoke with Mr. *Malloy*? About me going to see Mrs. *Ramondetta*?"

"It's school policy, Anna, to let parents know when their child has been to the counselor."

"Wow." This just keeps getting better.

"Not the specifics, of course, just the fact that you've met with her. And I think, well . . ." My father clears his throat. "Given everything that's happened . . . maybe it's not such a bad idea for you to talk to someone."

I take a sip of seltzer, shake my head. Take another sip.

"I know our last conversation wasn't . . . well, I didn't handle myself as well as I might have. I got . . . frustrated . . . talking about your mother. And I realize maybe that wasn't fair . . . to you. And I just wanted to say I'm sorry for losing my cool."

I stare at him. It's the second time this week my father has apologized to me.

"Huh," I say.

"Can you accept my apology?"

He's sorry for *losing his cool*. He's not apologizing for much, so there's not much to accept.

"Anna?"

I shrug.

"Is that a yes?" His face is pained, like this conversation is causing him actual, physical distress. Which makes me glad, in a way. Why should my mother be the only one who suffers?

"Anna," he says again. "Can you accept my apology?"

"I guess. Whatever."

"I'll take it." My father sighs, nods. He gives my shoulder an awkward pat. Pat, pat, pat. Pat, pat, pat. It's like Jane, patting *Goodnight Moon*.

"Okay, Dad," I say finally, taking a step back.

"Okay?"

"Yeah. Go watch your movie."

"You sure you don't want to watch with us?"

"I'm sure."

"Good night, Anna."

"Good night."

"Good night, Anna," Marnie says, suddenly appearing in the doorway. I swear to God that woman has bionic hearing.

"Good night," I say.

"I left something on your bed," she says.

"Okay."

Of course she left something on my bed. It is probably the new Pottery Barn teen catalog. Or paint samples. Because she *still* hasn't taken the hint that I will not be decorating that room.

But when I get upstairs, I see that I am wrong. It is not a Pottery Barn teen catalog. It is not paint samples. It is a plain manila envelope addressed to Ms. Anna Collette. It has "Lenox Park, Atlanta, Georgia" scrawled in the upper-left corner and "DO NOT BEND" scrawled across the top.

I grab a pair of scissors, slice open the envelope, pull out what's inside.

It's a photo.

It's a big, shiny, blown-up photo of Harper and Scarlett and Caro and Presley and Marnie and me. We are wearing our bedazzled tiger-paw tank tops. We have our arms around each other. Harper has half a hot dog hanging out of her mouth. Caro is crossing her eyes. Presley is grabbing Scarlett's boob and Marnie is giving me rabbit ears. We are all laughing.

Without even thinking, I open my backpack and pull out a roll of tape. I stick the photo on the wall next to my bed, so when I wake up it will be the first thing I see.

CHAPTER
19

IF YOU'D TOLD ME a year ago that I would be hanging out with Sarabeth Mueller and Shawna Wendall, I would have laughed. I didn't think we had anything in common. Maybe we still don't. But here we are.

The three of us have been brainstorming about our talent show act every day after school. Sarabeth has transformed her basement into a music studio. She even has microphones hooked up, and a stage area with mirrors on the wall so we can watch ourselves while we're singing.

It was Shawna who suggested we do a mash-up. Each of us picks a song and we find a way to mix them together, no matter how bizarre it sounds. We are, after all, Gobsmacked. We want to blow people's minds.

That's how we ended up with songs by Joan Jett, Sara

Bareilles, and Israel Kamakawiwo'ole—a random combination if ever there was one.

"An a cappella mash-up challenge," Sarabeth says, spreading out song lyrics on the floor. "Bring it."

I don't know why I ever thought Sarabeth was weird. I mean, she *is* weird, but not in a bad way. Here in her basement, her weirdness kind of makes her our leader.

"Where do we start?" Shawna says.

Sarabeth holds up a box of highlighters. "Common themes, common words, anything to connect these songs."

Shawna, despite her disdain for all things spirited, has become pretty gung ho about this talent show. It's strange. Every night this week, we've been talking on the phone—about our act, about Animal Planet, about music we like. Sometimes she'll throw in something serious when I least expect it. Like last night, I was talking to her from bed, and she just bluntly asked, "Is your mom bipolar one or bipolar two?"

"How did you know there are two?" I said.

"I read a lot of psych books, remember?" And she told me about this book, the *Diagnostic and Statistical Manual of Mental Disorders*, Fifth Edition, a diagnostic and statistical manual of mental disorders.

"You read that for *fun*?"

"Hello, I pluck out my own eyebrows. I read whatever I can to make sense of that."

I felt bad then, but Shawna didn't seem upset. She just asked me again. "So what is she—bipolar one or bipolar two?"

"Bipolar two," I said.

"Good. If you're going to be bipolar, that's the kind to be."

"Really?"

"Yup. It's much milder. Easier to treat. Better long-term prognosis."

"Huh."

She was quiet for a minute, and that's when I asked her. "So, what about you?"

"What about me?"

"You said you read those books to make sense of your . . . you know . . ."

"Trichotillomania?"

"Right."

"It's a mouthful, I know," Shawna said. "Most people just call it trich."

"Okay, trich. So how *do* you . . . make sense of it?"

"Well, I know I don't do it on purpose. That's the first thing. Trich is on the obsessive-compulsive spectrum. There are a few different theories. Brain abnormalities.

Gene mutations. Anxiety. Stress . . . I started pulling out my eyebrows when I was ten, right after my parents split up, so clearly that was a big stresser. But it's not the whole story."

"Can you . . . is there treatment?"

"Yeah," Shawna said. "There's behavioral therapy. And there's medication. Serotonin reuptake inhibitors. I do both. There's no *cure* exactly, but I can go into remission. That's, like, a break from the urge to pull them out, and then they can grow back in. Which I'm hoping will happen soon . . . Okay? Do you feel fully educated now?"

"Yes, I do," I said. "Thank you, Dr. Wendall."

"That'll be two hundred bucks," she said. "I'll have my office bill you."

Shawna is funny sometimes. Sarcastic, yes. Caustic, yes. But funny, too. Like now, in Sarabeth's basement, she is sprawled out on the floor, surrounded by paper and highlighters, and she is drawing a bicycle. "Pedal, boys!" she keeps shouting. Which is one of the lyrics to her song. It's called "Bad Reputation," and it's all about rebellion—going against the grain—which Shawna is so good at.

"I think I've got one," Sarabeth says, holding up a piece of paper. "Listen to this. *I've never been afraid . . . wanna see you be brave . . .* that fits right in with Anna's *dare to dream.* That's good, right?"

"Hell yeah," Shawna says.

"I like it," I say.

"Great," Sarabeth says. "Let the Gobsmacking begin!"

*　　*　　*

I didn't plan on doing this, but I'm doing this. As I leave Sarabeth's house, I call Marnie to let her know where I'm headed. She says fine, as long as I'm back before dark. It's mid-October, so the days are getting shorter. But luckily Sarabeth's house, Regina's house, and my dad's house are all along the same two-mile stretch, and there's a bike path.

It's cold and windy as I pedal up Regina's driveway. My mother is on the front stoop, huddled under a blanket, smoking a cigarette.

"Hey," I say.

She blows smoke off to one side. "Hey. This is unexpected."

I lean Marnie's bike against the house and walk up the steps. "I was in the neighborhood."

"Cold day for a bike ride," my mother says.

"It's not so bad."

I sit on the bench beside her. It's the first time I've seen her since that day in Regina's car. We've spoken on the phone a few times, but nothing face-to-face. She doesn't look much better, to be honest. Which means she still looks bad. Maybe her hair is less greasy, but she's pale, and she has on a ratty gray sweatshirt that must be Regina's because I've never seen it before.

"You came to see me," she says. "That's nice."

I nod but don't say anything. What is there to say? Does she care what I did today? Does she want to hear about Shawna's Joan Jett impersonation or Sarabeth's foot stomp that keeps the beat perfectly? Does she give a crap that we now have an awesome mash-up for the talent show? I don't know if she does. In a weird way, my mother feels like a stranger to me, even though I have known her my whole life. Even though we have laughed together and played Scrabble together and watched TV together and talked together about a million different subjects. Not just stupid stuff, either, like Dani and her mom, who always talked about diet tips and which celebrities were dating. My mom and I talked about important stuff. Like sex. And drugs. And peer pressure. And body image. And war in the Middle East. We have always been able to talk honestly about anything. Except for this. We do not talk about her depression. Not ever.

"Regina is making stuffed shells," she tells me.

"Yeah?" I love Regina's stuffed shells.

"Want to stay for dinner?"

"No," I lie.

She smiles a little. "Yes you do."

"We had stuffed shells the night before . . . everything happened . . . remember? You wouldn't get out of bed, so Regina dropped off food."

My mother takes a drag of her cigarette.

"You wouldn't eat, either," I say. "I had to eat by myself."

She closes her eyes, blows out a stream of smoke. "God, I sound like a delinquent mother."

I shake my head and shrug. I think about telling her she's not, but I'd only be saying it to make her feel better. So I don't.

"You know how depression hits?" She takes another drag and blows the smoke out slowly. "It's like an avalanche. No warning. You're just knocked off your feet. You reach for a ledge . . . no ledge. You reach for a branch . . . no branch. You just keep falling. When you hit the bottom, everything around you settles like concrete. You're up to your neck and you can't move. All you can do is wait."

"For what? A rescue dog?" The words come out sarcastic, but she doesn't seem to notice.

She shakes her head. "No one can rescue you. You're on your own. You have to look for a foothold."

"But you're trapped in concrete," I remind her.

"You have to wait for it to crack. Then you have to chip your way out. *Then* you look for a foothold."

"Oh."

My mother glances at me. "Do you think," she says quietly, "that you'll forgive me sometime?"

Forgive her for what? I wonder. For trying to kill herself? For trying to kill herself in a place where I would find her? For not staying on her medication, which might have kept her from trying to kill herself in the first place? There is so much to forgive.

"I don't know," I say. "Will there be another avalanche?"

My mother crushes her cigarette in one of Regina's flowerpots. "I can't promise you there won't."

"Then I can't promise I'll forgive you." It comes out bitchy, which isn't how I mean it. What I mean is, *Please don't try it again.*

She takes a pack of Marlboro Lights out of her sweat-shirt. "The doctors are hopeful. It's a new diagnosis. New medication."

"Are you *taking* it?"

She nods.

"Are you going to *stay on it*?"

She lets out a sigh. "I'm going to try, Anna. I'm really going to try this time." She shakes the pack. "I'm out of the concrete. I've got my first foothold. That's all I can tell you right now."

I nod. There's nothing else I can ask for, no contract I can make her sign. So we just sit there on the bench. She takes out another cigarette, lights it. We watch the orange and red and gold leaves swirl around Regina's yard.

"I'm glad you're feeling better," I finally say.

"Me too."

"It's getting dark." I stand up. "I should go."

She nods. I bend over and kiss her cheek. Then I head down the stairs and hop on Marnie's bike.

*   *   *

When I get back, Marnie is in the kitchen. She has Jane in the BabyBjörn and there is flour everywhere. Flour on the counters, flour on the floor, flour on Marnie's cheek, flour in Jane's hair. "Hey, Anna." Marnie smiles when she sees me. "Jane and I are baking!"

"I can see that."

"Try this," she says, handing me something.

"What is it?"

"It's a muffin."

"It's *green*."

"I know. I call it the Incredible Hulk."

I lift the muffin to my nose, sniff. "There's no kale in this thing, is there?"

"Don't worry about what's in it. Just try it."

I take a bite. I don't want to, but I do. I chew, chew. Swallow.

"Well?"

"It's not bad, actually."

"Really?"

"Really." I'm not lying. I take another bite.

"Did you hear that, Janie? Your sister likes our muffins!" When Marnie claps, a puff of flour hits the air.

CHAPTER
20

MY FATHER AND JANE walk me to the bus stop in the morning, which is totally unnecessary and weird. It is doubly weird because my father is wearing sweatpants. Marnie is sick, apparently, and he is staying home to help out.

"She was fine yesterday," I say. "She was making muffins."

"She was vomiting all night."

"Bummer."

"Yeah. Do you need money for lunch?"

"I'm good."

"You sure? I'll just give you a ten . . ." He tries to reach into his pocket, then realizes he's wearing sweatpants.

"It's okay. I already packed a lunch."

"You did?" He sounds surprised.

"Dad. I've been packing my own lunches since I was, like, seven."

"You have?"

"Are you seriously pretending you don't know that?"

"I'm not pretending anything."

"Well, I did. I cooked, too. And did laundry. And rolled Mom out of bed and stuck her in the shower."

My father frowns. "I don't remember that."

"That's because you were never home."

"I must have been working."

"Whatever," I mutter.

"Don't *whatever* me, Anna. I don't appreciate it."

"Well, I don't *appreciate* your selective memory."

My father shakes his head. "I don't want to fight with you."

"You think I want to fight with *you*?"

"I don't know." He huffs out a sigh, shifts Jane from one arm to the other. There's a string of drool hanging from her bottom lip, threatening to drop. "Marnie thinks—"

"Oh, *Marnie* thinks? What does *Marnie* think?"

"She thinks you and I need to work on communicating more effectively."

"Really," I say.

"Yes."

"Well, that is an astute observation."

"Are you being sarcastic? I can't tell."

"I don't know," I say. "Maybe. Probably."

"Rotten teenager."

"Rotten father."

It is the weirdest thing, the tiniest lifting of tension. So tiny. A smirk twitching at both our mouths, just as the bus pulls up.

*　　*　　*

"Hey, Anna," Sarabeth says when I plop down next to her.

"Hey."

"Talent-show shopping today. Did you bring money?"

"Yup." I pat my pocket.

After school, Mrs. Mueller is taking Sarabeth, Shawna, and me to Roz's Place in North Providence, to find clothes for our act. I've never been there, but apparently it's a thrift store with really cool, inexpensive clothes.

"There's something for everyone," Sarabeth says. "Preppy. Goth. Emo. Skater. Punk. Euro. Hippie. You name it."

"I don't know what I am," I say.

Sarabeth grins. "That's the fun part."

*　　*　　*

The school day drags. It always does, but anticipation of a shopping spree makes it move even slower than usual.

The only person who has ever taken me to buy clothes is my mother, and she has such strong opinions that it's not even fun. *I don't want you to be a slave to fashion, Anna,* she would say. And, *Your worth should not be defined by what you wear.* Hence my no-name jeans and granny panties. I never got to decide who I was because my mother wouldn't let me step foot in the stores where other girls shopped. *Those mannequins look like child prostitutes. Do you want to look like a child prostitute, Anna?* The one time I went to the mall with Dani and came home with a halter top, my mother made me return it. When I pointed out her hypocrisy—she had a closet full of halter tops—she didn't even blink. *I'm an adult. You're a child. I want you to think about the message you're sending.*

Well, the message I'm sending today is *Ha!* The school counselor won't be there to judge. It'll just be me, and my pocketful of cash—the sum total of the money my father has given me since I moved in.

"Anna?"

I look up. "Yeah?"

Ms. Baer-Leighton smiles. She has something brown and crusty-looking in the corner of her mouth. Chocolate, maybe. Or refried beans. I can hear sniggering and

I don't even have to turn around to see who it is. Jessa Bell and Whitney Anderson spend half of every class mocking people.

"Do you have an answer to number seven?" Ms. Baer-Leighton says, and there it is, staring at me. The brown shmutz.

"Thirteen degrees," I tell her.

When everyone else is working on number eight, I find myself walking over to Ms. Baer-Leighton's desk, pretending I need her help with the problem. *You have something on your face*, I write on a piece of paper.

She reads what I've written and nods. A few minutes later, she excuses herself to go to the bathroom. When she gets back, the brown stuff is gone, and I'm glad. I know kids make fun of Ms. Baer-Leighton all the time, because of her hair and her clothes. But I don't care what she looks like. No one deserves to walk around all day with refried beans on her face.

* * *

Mrs. Mueller drops us off at Roz's Place. She's dying to come with us, I can tell, but Sarabeth insists that she go get coffee.

Inside, there are racks and racks of clothes. Jeans, dresses, jackets, vests. Boots, belts, scarves, and earrings.

It's a treasure trove of fashion. The woman folding a pile of sweaters introduces herself as Roz. Spiky purple hair. Thigh-high boots. Lip ring. I don't know what her look is—Punk? Emo?—but it's definitely not Shelby Horner cheerleader.

"Poke around, girls," she tells us, sweeping a bangled arm through the air. "If you need any help, holler."

This is the opposite of the guy at the indie music store Keesha Soboleski and I used to go to. He always assumed we were going to steal something and made us leave our backpacks at the counter.

"Could you point me toward the capes?" Sarabeth says.

And Shawna says, "Could you point me *away* from the capes?"

"Free to be you and me," Sarabeth says.

"Okay, Gloria Steinem."

"Come with me," Roz tells Sarabeth.

"I'm starting upstairs," Shawna tells me.

"There's an upstairs?"

Having so much to choose from is hard. You need to narrow things down. Do you want a poncho? A corduroy blazer? Go-go boots?

I wander aimlessly, until Roz puts on some music. "To aid in the shopping experience," she tells us. "Channel your inner Gaga, darlings. Clothes aren't just for dressing up. They're for *transforming*."

It's funny, how the music makes a difference. We start pulling stuff off racks for each other. We pick things never before seen in the halls of Shelby Horner Middle School. The rule is, whatever someone hands you, you have to put on. We try to outdo each other with our outrageous finds. Platform Chuck Taylors. Vinyl pants with cats embroidered on the knees. A hamburger-print dress. A green, polyester jumpsuit. We parade up and down the stairs, cracking each other up with our model poses. At one point, Shawna jumps out of the dressing room in a leather jacket, red jeans with rips all over the place, and studded black biker boots. "This . . ." she says, "you gotta admit . . . is badass."

We give her a round of applause.

"Let's find you a black bandana for your wrist," Roz says. "And maybe a chain or two . . ."

By the time Mrs. Mueller comes back, Sarabeth has decided against the cape. She has found a pink satin bomber jacket and bowling shoes instead.

I don't think I will find anything. I have almost given up hope when Shawna sweeps down the stairs, holding something behind her back. *"Some . . . wherrrrre . . . oooooover the rainbowwww . . ."*

Obviously, whatever she has found is for me because this is my song.

"Anna." She is smiling.

"What?"

"I have something for you . . . This is so good. I want to make sure you're prepared for how good it is."

"Just show me."

"May I present . . ." She pauses dramatically. "The vintage seventies . . . hand-crocheted . . . rainbow halter dress!" And she whips it out.

Is it perfect?

It is so perfect.

It gets more applause than Shawna's leather jacket. Even Sarabeth's mom is enraptured. She squeezes my arm. "If you don't buy that dress, Anna, *I* will buy it for myself."

"She will, too," Sarabeth says. "Save me, Anna. Save us all."

"I love it," I say.

*   *   *

We're hyper on the way out of the store. I'm wearing the hippie headband Roz threw in for free—rawhide with crocheted daisies. We're all laughing and singing Lady Gaga songs and bumping each other's hips as we walk down the sidewalk. I'm having such a good time that I don't notice right away. I mean I *see* that two people are walking toward us, but it takes me a second to process.

At first I'm confused. *This can't be*, I think.

And then it hits me. Dani's orthodontist is in North Providence, in this very neighborhood. I went with her to get her braces off.

"Well, look who it is," Mrs. Loomis calls out. "Look, Danielle, it's Anna! Hi, Anna! We were just getting Danielle's new retainer."

Nope. My eyes aren't deceiving me.

Dani looks at me and her cheeks turn blotchy red. "Hey."

And I say, " 'Sup."

I don't think I've ever said *'sup* in my life, but that's what comes out.

It's a weird moment, made even weirder by the fact that Dani doesn't acknowledge anyone else; she just keeps walking. I catch a whiff of her green apple shampoo, and a hundred little memories flash through my head. Me and Dani washing our Barbies. Me and Dani baking brownies. Me and Dani playing spit. Me and Dani talking. Me and Dani dancing. Me and Dani laughing hysterically. I feel a prick of sadness, and then, as quickly as it came, it's gone.

*   *   *

When I get back, Marnie is in the kitchen, gagging over a plate of chicken thighs.

"Are you okay?"

She gives me a watery smile. "I can't deal with raw meat right now."

I look around. "Where's my dad?"

"He took Jane out to do errands. I wanted to have dinner ready when they got back, but—" She pokes a piece of chicken, gags again.

"Want me to do it?"

"Would you?"

"Go lie down," I tell her. "I'll make dinner."

"Really?"

"Really," I say. I look at Marnie, whose face has a greenish tinge. "Stomach bugs are the worst, huh?"

She nods shakily. "I *hate* throwing up."

"Me too."

It's the weirdest thing, after she leaves. A déjà-vu feeling but not. I find myself alone in the kitchen making dinner, but for once in my life, I'm not worried about the sick mother upstairs. What I'm doing—putting on an apron, setting the oven for 350—actually means something.

In a little while, my dad walks into the kitchen with Jane in the Björn. Their cheeks are pink from the cold.

"Anna," he says, surprised. "You're cooking."

"Yeah. So?"

"It smells good."

"It should. It's barbecue chicken and corn bread."

"Barbecue chicken and corn bread?" He rubs his hands together. "You hear that, Janie? Your sister's a gourmet."

I roll my eyes. "It's no big deal."

He reaches into the salad bowl, grabs a crouton, and pops it in his mouth.

"Hey!" I say. "We're eating in fifteen minutes!"

"All right. All right." He starts to unstrap Jane.

"Here." I reach out my hands. "I'll take her. You go wash up and check on Marnie."

My father looks surprised again.

"What? You think I can't hold a baby?" I lift Jane out of his arms and prop her on my hip like a koala bear.

"The sauce is from a jar," I whisper into her soft hair, "and the corn bread's from a mix. But Daddy doesn't have to know."

She looks up at me and smiles. Then she lets out a big fart.

"Nice," I tell her. "Real classy."

CHAPTER
21

I'M SPENDING MORE and more time at Sarabeth's. Mostly it's her, Shawna, and me rehearsing. We work on harmonies and choreography. We practice solos. We record ourselves and play it back, looking for ways to improve. Other times, we just hang out. Do our homework. Listen to music. Eat junk.

The week before Halloween, Shawna opens a cabinet in the basement and finds all of Sarabeth's old dolls— the ones that used to be up in her bedroom. She says, "Holy crap, S.B." (This is what Shawna has taken to calling Sarabeth: *S.B.*) "What *are* these?"

"Collector's items," Sarabeth says. "My grandmother gave them to me."

"We have to do something with them," Shawna says.

"Like what?"

"I don't know. Something."

And Shawna comes up with this crazy idea to dress the dolls in costumes and put them out on the Muellers' front porch, to scare the trick-or-treaters. At first Sarabeth doesn't go for it. She thinks her grandmother would be mad. But then she admits that she's never liked these dolls anyway; they give her the creeps.

So we go to work. Sarabeth busts out the toilet paper and felt and masking tape. We make a mummy, a zombie, a devil, and a werewolf. We make a headless horseman and a bride of Frankenstein. We bring the dolls outside and take a bunch of stupid pictures of ourselves holding them, and we laugh like idiots.

Sometimes I look at these girls and think, okay, they are so weird. Other times they surprise me. Like when Sarabeth confessed that she hates her name, and on her eighteenth birthday she wants to change it to Sadie San Marco. Or when Shawna told me that her dad's a plastic surgeon. He gets paid a ridiculous amount of money to make women look like supermodels, and he keeps offering to "fix" Shawna. Every time he offers, she does something that she knows he will hate. She dyes her hair black. She pierces her belly button. Sarabeth and Shawna are a lot more interesting than I ever gave them credit for. Weird, yes. But not in a bad way.

Mostly, I am just glad they're here. My mother is no

longer consuming my every thought. I am too busy to spend every waking moment agonizing about her. Is she eating enough? Is she smoking too much? Is she taking her medicine? I can't worry every two seconds that she's going to kill herself. There's school. There's rehearsal. There's homework. There's Friday-night football. There's a sleepover at Reese's. There's the Jack-o'-Lantern Spectacular at the Roger Williams Park Zoo. This is how it goes as we head into November. And suddenly, it's talent show time.

I call Regina's house on November 1. Until now, I have avoided mentioning the talent show. The conversations I've had with my mother have been short. *How are you feeling?* I ask. *Better,* she says. *How's school?* she asks. *Okay,* I say. Twice, Regina has had me over for dinner, but she is the one who does all the talking. My mom and I are careful with each other. She is careful, I think, because she doesn't want to worry me. I am careful because I don't want to worry. Which is why I don't bring up the talent show until three days before. There's a part of me that doesn't actually want her to come. If I wait until the last second, maybe she and Regina will have other plans.

"Anna Banana!" Regina says when she answers.

"Hey," I say.

"How are you, honey?"

"I'm good."

"Good, good. What's on tap for the weekend?"

"Actually, that's why I'm calling . . . What are you and my mom doing Friday night?"

"Nothing."

"Oh." My stomach drops a little. "Okay." I lower my voice, even though my mother can't hear me. "Do you think she's okay to come out in public?"

"Why don't you ask her yourself?"

"No. I want you to tell me what you—"

"Frannie!" But Regina is already calling my mother. "Fran! Anna's on the phone!"

There's some shuffling around in the background. Then, "Anna?"

"Hi, Mom."

"Everything okay?"

"Yeah. How are you?"

"I'm doing okay."

Really? I think. *How okay is okay?*

"Um . . . listen," I say before I can change my mind. "I'm in this talent show thing on Friday night and I'm calling to see if you and Regina want to come."

Silence.

"Mom?"

"You're in a talent show?"

"Yeah. I'm singing. With two other girls."

Another silence. Bigger this time. Then, "Oh, Anna, I would *love* to come."

Her voice is wavery with emotion.

"Are you sure?" I am already regretting it.

"Yes."

"Because if you're still . . . you know . . . you don't have to . . ."

"I wouldn't miss it."

"Okay . . . well, great. Put Regina on and I'll give her the info."

*   *   *

I can't believe tonight is the night. Giddiness overtakes me as the three of us crowd around Sarabeth's mirror to see how we look. Did we practice enough? Are we as good as we think we are? I feel a little sick to my stomach, but it's not all about getting up onstage and singing in front of hundreds of people. It's about my mother being there. What was I thinking, inviting her? Just because she *seems* better doesn't mean she *is*. She could still do something embarrassing.

Shawna is pushing on my arm, trying to get closer to the mirror. Sarabeth is behind me with the straightening iron, working on my hair.

"I'm nervous," I announce.

"Nerves are good," Sarabeth says.

"I might barf."

She hands me a trash can. "Here."

For a second I think I really might. But then I take a deep breath, and the moment passes.

"I'm okay now," I say.

Sarabeth pats my shoulder. She is as cool as can be. She's used to performing in Irish step competitions, so tonight is no big deal. Her job is to keep me and Shawna composed.

"If I get detention for singing my song right, you're both coming with me," Shawna mutters.

At tech rehearsal, Shawna was told she would need to change the lyric "I don't give a damn" to "I don't give a *hoot.*" Why? Because Shelby Horner is a "profanity-free school."

Thankfully, Shawna didn't make a stink about it to Mr. Winters, the drama director. She waited until afterward to tell us that (a) "damn" is not a swear word—blasphemous, maybe, but not indecent—and (b) she is going to do Joan Jett proud, no matter the consequences.

"Don't worry, Joan," Sarabeth says. "If you go down, we all go down. Right, Anna?"

"Damn right," I say.

Shawna gives me a sloppy-wet smooch on the cheek. "Eww."

"Accept the love, woman."

*   *   *

"Are we ready?" Sarabeth asks. "Are we pumped?" We are out in the hall, and she is walking back and forth between me and Shawna, rubbing our shoulders like we're the Outsiders, getting ready to rumble.

"We're gonna be great," Shawna says, bouncing up and down on the toes of her biker boots.

"Of course we are," Sarabeth says, and I can tell she's enjoying the looks we're getting from the ninth-grade boys who just walked by.

"We *have* to be better than Beyoncé and the Bobbleheads," Shawna says.

"Hey, now," Sarabeth says. "That was technical difficulties."

It was so cringeworthy, watching Jessa Bell, Whitney Anderson, and Dani stumble around the stage in their platform heels, wearing way too much makeup and way too few clothes. Their lip-synching to "Single Ladies" was painful enough, but when someone backstage tripped over the extension cord and unplugged the speakers, the three of them just froze. Some boys in the crowd booed. I almost felt sorry for Dani. Almost.

We walk through the stage door and gather behind the curtain. There's one more act before ours: two seventh-grade boys with yo-yos. They are really good. Yo-yos fly everywhere—over their heads, behind their backs. The yo-yo-ers move all over the stage. One of them even does a cartwheel without dropping his yo-yo. When they finish, Shawna sticks her fingers in her mouth and whistles louder than anything I've ever heard.

Sarabeth and I turn and stare at her.

She shrugs. "My dad taught me."

Before we can find out how she does it, we hear the MCs—two ninth-grade girls in sequined hats—announce us, and bam—here we are onstage. Sarabeth is blowing her pitch pipe, and her feet are starting to stomp, and Shawna is sneering like a rebel, and the lights are bright and the air is hot, and for a second I think I might pass out.

But then I open my mouth.

It's hard to describe how it feels up there. The whole space is ours, and, even though the words aren't really ours, we own them right now. We've put them together in our own patchwork way. We are brave, we are rebels, we are dreamers who dare to dream. Our voices are pure and strong and open and defiant. I can smell the leather of Shawna's jacket and the wax of Sarabeth's lipstick as we dance around each other. When I break out of the group to sing my solo, I think I spot my mother in the crowd—a shock of black hair, a green shirt—but then I lose her. I lift my chin and let the words soar out over everyone's heads. High and sweet, shimmering like lemon drops.

That's where . . .

you'll . . .

find me . . .

I forget to be nervous. I forget that my mother is watching. It's just me, right here, all lit up.

When I stop singing there's a beat of silence, then applause.

Chloe, Nicole, and Reese are going nuts. Some of the ninth-grade boys in the front row are doing that slow-motion, sarcastic clap thing, but I don't care. No one is booing. No one is laughing as far as I can tell. Sarabeth and Shawna and I hold hands, bow, lift our arms in the air, bow again. There's another act after ours, but I don't want to leave. I want to rewind time and do it all over again.

*   *   *

Afterward, the lobby is packed. Just when I think I'll never find anyone, Regina grabs me and puts me in a headlock.

"You were staggeringly good," she says. My face is smashed into her chest, which smells like tomato sauce. "I am staggered."

When I come up for air, there is my mother. The first thing I should say is that she looks good. The best she has looked in a long time. Her hair is smooth. She's wearing lipstick. A green silk shirt. Who would have thought she'd go to this much effort for a Shelby Horner Middle School talent show?

I let her hug me.

"You look so grown-up," she murmurs. "When did that happen?"

When you were stuck in concrete, I think. *I've aged ten years in the past six weeks.* But I tell her, "It's just the dress."

Then I hear my father's voice behind me, and I'm glad because it gives me an excuse to turn around.

"Wow." My dad pats my shoulder, over and over. "Just . . . wow."

"You liked it?"

He nods.

"Really?"

"I loved it," he says firmly. To my mother he says, "Hello, Fran."

"Hello, David."

They do a weird, polite cheek kiss thing.

It's awkward for a moment. Then my dad says something that kills me. "She looked like you up there."

"You think so?" my mother says.

"Spitting image."

It's good to see my mom smile, but then Regina has to go and ruin it. "Where's your wife, Dave-O?" she says. "Is it past her bedtime?"

"She's home with the baby," my dad says, ignoring the barb. He looks at his watch. "I should be getting back . . . Anna? You coming with me?"

I remind him that I'm sleeping at Sarabeth's tonight. Her mom will drop me off in the morning. "Thanks, Dad," I tell him, "for coming."

"Wouldn't have missed it," he says, and squeezes my arm.

After he leaves, Mr. Pfaff appears out of nowhere. It's the first time I've ever seen him in jeans.

"Anna . . . you were great."

"Thanks," I say.

"Really great. I didn't know you could sing."

I shrug. There's a lot Mr. Pfaff doesn't know about me.

I am trying to think of a way to free myself from this

conversation when I notice Mr. Pfaff noticing my mom. I am ever so slightly horrified when he says, "Frannie? . . . Frannie Whipple?"

My mother looks at him. "I'm sorry. Do I—"

"Peter." He points to his chest. "Pfaffenbichler . . . Staples High School? *Inklings?*"

Something clicks into place and my mom's mouth drops open. "Oh my God." To Regina she explains, "Pete and I worked on the school newspaper together, a hundred years ago." They go through the whole how-long-have-you-lived-here, how-did-we-not-know-this routine, and then Mr. Pfaff says, "You haven't changed a bit."

"*You* have." She grabs hold of his goatee. "What's this?"

His face turns pink.

My mom smiles. "I like it."

"You do?"

"I do. You look like a journalist."

Now he's smiling, too. Wait—are they *flirting*? Please tell me that my mother and my English teacher are not *sharing a moment*. This is too *Twilight Zone* for words.

Luckily, Shawna grabs my arm and drags me away. "He did it," she says.

"Who did what?"

"Mr. Winters. He gave me three days' detention for saying *damn*."

"Don't worry," I tell her. "We'll do it with you."

"I'm not worried." Shawna laughs. "I don't even care! My dad will be pissed because I'm making him look bad, and he and my mom will have a huge fight about whether or not to ground me, but since he didn't come tonight, he won't know until Winters calls him—"

"Your dad didn't come?"

Shawna snorts. "Ha!"

"Why *ha*?"

"Are you kidding? It's my mom's weekend. My parents can't be in the same room for more than five minutes or they start throwing things."

I nod. "Rough." It occurs to me that my parents did pretty well tonight, considering. Maybe it's because Marnie didn't come. Maybe it's because my mom is actually taking her medicine. It doesn't really matter what the reason is. I'm just glad, in a weird way, that they were both here.

"Whatever," Shawna says. "I don't care if my dad's mad. It was worth it. This is the best night of my life! . . . Come on." She grabs my hand. "Let's go find Sarabeth."

*   *   *

She looked like you up there. You think so? Spitting image.
All night at Sarabeth's house, the words whisper in my

head. It's the nicest thing my father has said to my mother in a long time. He made her smile tonight, and I don't know why, but it feels like a good omen.

The three of us lie on the floor in Sarabeth's basement, eating popcorn and talking. About everything. Teachers we like. Teachers we can't stand. Boys we'd kiss. Boys we wouldn't touch with a ten-foot pole. We have a heated discussion about whether the boys who were mean in elementary school could eventually become nice boyfriends.

"Everyone's capable of change," Sarabeth says.

"No way," Shawna says. "Once a jackass, always a jackass."

"What about Inspector Gustav, from *Hugo*?" I say. "He's the ultimate jackass until he falls in love."

"Or Snape, from *Harry Potter*," Sarabeth chimes in. "Everyone thinks he's bad, but really, he's just heartbroken."

"Or Mr. Pfaff—" Shawna says.

I whack her with a pillow.

"Hey!" Shawna whacks me back. "He could be the best boyfriend ever, you don't know. He could be your mom's true love."

I stare at her. "I don't want my mom to have a *boyfriend*."

"Why not?"

237

"I want her to focus on getting well."

Sarabeth smiles. "Maybe Mr. Pfaff is the best medicine."

"Please," I snort.

"He can read Shakespeare to her," Shawna says. "He can recite *sonnets*."

"Any day now," I say, "you'll shut up about Mr. Pfaff and my mom."

Shawna smiles wider.

Sarabeth giggles.

I whack them both with a pillow. "I will never. Tell you guys. Anything. Again."

"Sure you will," Shawna says.

"You love us," Sarabeth says.

When Sarabeth turns out the lights and our voices fade into silence, I lie there in the dark thinking, *I love these freaks.*

Maybe Sarabeth is right after all. Maybe everyone is capable of change.

CHAPTER
22

MARNIE AND MY FATHER are both in the kitchen when Mrs. Mueller drops me off. Jane is in her high chair, gumming on a teething biscuit.

"How was your sleepover?" my dad says, giving me a clap on the back.

"Fine," I say.

"I heard you were amazing last night," Marnie says. She turns to my dad. "What was that word you used, honey? Radiant?"

"Luminous."

Marnie's head bobs up and down. "*Luminous* . . . that's right . . . well, I'm sorry I missed it, Anna. I hope someone took video."

"Mrs. Mueller did," I say.

"Great! Will you ask her to email it to me?"

"Uh . . . sure."

"Marnie's muffins were very popular, by the way," my dad says.

"What?"

"The muffins she baked. For the concession stand."

Right. I forgot about Marnie's muffins because she didn't come to the talent show. My dad delivered them for her.

"Everyone was raving." My dad puts his arm around Marnie. She looks at him. He squeezes her shoulders.

I'm getting a weird vibe here. I can't put my finger on it, but I feel like I'm watching a play.

"We should celebrate!" my dad suddenly exclaims. He whips around to the refrigerator and pulls out a bottle of sparkling cider. "Martinelli's apple-pear . . . Rhode Island's finest!"

That's when it hits me: I've heard these lines before.

It's like a sucker punch, the feeling. I close my eyes. *Fine*, I think. *It's going to be fine.*

"You okay, kiddo?" my father asks.

I nod.

Marnie is opening the cabinet, taking down wine glasses.

Of course, I think. *The puking. The raw chicken . . . First we're going to toast the talent show, and then they're going to tell me she's pregnant.*

"I have to go to the bathroom," I blurt.

My dad smiles and pops off the top. "Can you give us a minute?"

I nod dumbly. I watch him pour the cider. I take the glass he offers me.

Just rip off the Band-Aid, I think. One baby, two babies, does it really matter? I was never going to live here permanently; it was just a place to sleep while my mother was in the hospital. Soon we'll be back to Wednesday nights and every other weekend. So why do I feel so sad?

"A toast," my father says, raising his glass. "To my beautiful, talented daughter."

"Hear, hear," Marnie says.

We clink glasses.

"I'm proud of you, Anna," my dad says. "I know this hasn't been an easy time for you—"

"It's been fine," I murmur. "I'm fine."

"You're better than fine," Marnie says. "You're great. You've been a huge help to me—especially these past few weeks . . ."

"I really have to go to the bathroom," I choke out. I turn and run out of the kitchen.

"Anna?" my dad calls after me. "You okay?"

"Fine!" I manage to call back. "Just give me a few minutes!" And I sprint, as fast as I can, through the house and out the front door.

There is only one place I want to be right now, and that is in my own bed, in my own house, and I won't stop pedaling until I get there.

The key is where it always is, under the loose brick on the patio. You have to wiggle the knob to open the front door. I haven't forgotten.

I step inside, smell my house smell, see the funky antique hat rack and the gray flannel couch and the framed picture of the three dancing cats on the wall, and immediately start sobbing. I sob and sob, like a little kid. Tears, tears, tears—and it's not just about another baby. It's about everything. All the old hurts that led me to this point. I run upstairs and fling myself down on my bed and cry, thinking, *Why did my dad leave? Why weren't we enough?* And when I'm all cried out, I close my eyes and sleep.

*　　*　　*

I don't know how it happens, but when I wake up, my mother is sitting on the edge of my bed.

"Hey," she says softly. "I thought I might find you here."

Just seeing her face makes me cry all over. She puts her arms around me and doesn't say a word.

"Marnie's pregnant," I say finally, mopping my face with my sleeve. "Again."

"She is?"

I nod.

"Your father didn't mention that."

"You talked to Dad?"

"He was worried about you. He didn't know where you went. He said you left to go to the bathroom and you never came back."

"He didn't tell you about Marnie?"

"No."

"They were just about to make the big announcement. They had sparkling cider, just like last time . . . and I couldn't . . . I just had to get out of there."

My mother nods.

"How did you know where to find me?"

"I'm your mom," she says, smoothing back the hair from my face. "I'll always know where to find you." She sits there, looking all maternal, and it suddenly makes me mad.

I pull away from her.

"Are you . . ." She folds her hands in her lap. "Do you think you're ready to come home?"

"Are *you*?"

"I think so. Yeah. I'm shooting for next weekend. What do you say?"

"I don't know," I mumble.

There's an expression on her face I can't exactly read. Sadness mixed with disappointment mixed with something else.

"I understand," she says softly.

"It's just . . . you look better *now*. You're saying all the right things *now* . . . but what happens when we come back here? What happens in a week? What happens in a month? Am I going to wake up in the middle of the night and find you cleaning the kitchen with Q-tips? Or, worse . . ." I look around the room, throw my arms in the air. "Hanging from a ceiling fan?"

She doesn't answer at first. I watch her blink and swallow. "What do you want me to do, Anna?"

"I can't find you like that again. Don't put me in that position. I can't be worrying all the time that my mother is going to kill herself." The words are tumbling out of my mouth like hot coals, burning my tongue. "It's not my job to worry about you. It's *your* job . . . *you're* the parent . . . you can't . . . you *need* to stay on your medication, because if you go off . . . you'll have no one to blame but yourself."

"I know," she says, looking down at her hands.

I'm sorry, I almost say. *I'm sorry I said that.* Except I'm not sorry. I meant every word.

"I haven't been a perfect mother, but I swear, Anna, I'm trying."

"I know, Mom."

"I love you."

"I know."

"Will you at least think about what I said?" Her eyes soften as she looks at me. "About moving back?"

"I'll think about it."

"Thank you."

I let her hug me for a minute. Then I pull away.

"I should go, though, okay? If Dad's worried."

She nods. "I'll walk you out."

*   *   *

By the time I get back, it's dark, and I hope that my father and Marnie are upstairs in bed. But no such luck. My father is on the porch, sitting on the top step.

Crap, I think, leaning Marnie's bike against the side of the house. *Crap, crap, crap.* I walk slowly up the front walk.

"Anna," my father says.

"Congratulations," I mumble, but I can't look at him. I focus my attention on the bottom step.

"Honey, it's not—"

I hold up my hand. "Please don't say anything. I figured it out. And I'm sorry I took off, but I just couldn't—"

"Marnie's not pregnant."

I look up. *"What?"*

"Your mother called. She said you told her Marnie was pregnant. And I'm telling you she's not."

"Are you serious?"

"Yes."

"Marnie's not pregnant?"

"No."

"So, what—?"

"She's starting her own business. That's what we were going to tell you. Marnie's Muffins."

"Marnie's Muffins," I repeat.

"Healthy versions of your favorite baked goods. Delivered right to your door."

"Oh," I say. "Oh."

"She said she got the idea from you. From some show you were watching together?"

"Cupcake Wars," I murmur. I'm still staring at the bottom step.

"Come here," my father says. He pats the space beside him and I sit. My heart is thudding in my chest. I don't know if it's from shock or relief.

We're quiet for a minute. Both of us looking out at the yard, listening to the stillness.

"I fainted when you were born," my dad says. "Did I ever tell you that? The second I saw your face, I passed out cold."

I shake my head. "You never told me."

"You were so beautiful I couldn't breathe. Technicolor. Covered in slime . . . the loudest cry I ever heard . . . I looked at you and time stopped."

"Please."

"It's true."

I roll my eyes.

"You can ask your mother," my dad says. "After I came to, I held you in my arms and I said, *My life will never be the same. I'm a dad.*"

"Stop it," I say.

"You think I'm making this up," my father says. "I'm not. Nothing changes a person more than becoming a parent . . . You, Anna Sophia Collette, changed everything."

I look down at my shoes. "I did?"

"You did. And so did Jane. And, if Marnie *were* to get pregnant again, which she is *not*, but if she were, that baby would change everything, too."

"Well," I say, trying not to sound like a snotty teenager,

"that'll be great. Then you can give the new baby my room."

My dad looks at me, frowning. "Who said anything about giving up your room?"

"No one. I just assume, if there's ever a new baby . . ."

"Anna. You really think I would kick you out of your room? I told you the day we moved in, that room is yours."

"Yeah, well, you only have three bedrooms."

"So?"

"What about Marnie's business?"

"What about it?"

"Won't she need a space?"

"She'll have the kitchen. And she can share my office if she needs to. We'll manage, okay?"

I nod.

"Okay?" he says again.

"Okay."

"Come on." He stands up, turns toward the house. "There are some strange-looking muffins sitting on the kitchen counter. I'll warm one up for you."

CHAPTER
23

"HEY, ANNA."

I turn my head. Ethan Zane is looking at me and it takes a second to realize that he is the one who is talking. To me.

I glance around the English room to see if this is a joke, but no one is laughing. No one is even looking at us except for Dani.

"Hey," I say.

He squints, reminding me of his superlative in our seventh-grade yearbook: "Class Eyes." Ethan Zane has chameleon eyes. When he wears green, they are green. When he wears blue, they are blue. They even change in the light. A girl could get hypnotized looking at those eyes.

"Nice job in the talent show," he says, cocking his

head at me like I am some exotic bird he has noticed for the first time, even though we have known each other since kindergarten. Which, come to think of it, is probably the last time he talked to me. Pathetic.

I lift my chin, say, "Thanks."

"You surprised us up there," Dani chimes in. "You haven't been onstage since what—fifth grade?"

"Something like that." I squint down at the short story Mr. Pfaff photocopied for everyone and asked us to discuss while he talks to someone in the hall. "This is like eight-point font. How are we supposed to read this?"

"I'm trying to give you a compliment, Anna."

I look up. "Is that what you're doing?"

"Yes." Dani is frowning, which I know means she's annoyed that I'm not giving her 100 percent of my attention. "You were good."

"Thank you."

"It made me hate you a little."

I raise my eyebrows.

"Ethan thought you sang like Katy Perry."

"Ha!" I snort.

"You did," Ethan says, shrugging. "Looked like her, too."

I try not to snort again, but it just slips out.

"Just take the compliment," Dani mutters. "God."

I look at her, wondering if she's jealous, because that is how she sounds. Which makes me want to laugh. *Am I cool enough to be friends with you now?* I think about asking Dani this question—how much it would annoy her—but then I decide it's not worth it.

"You seem different, you know?" she says quietly.

"How's that?"

She shakes her head. "I don't know."

"I'm not the one who changed," I remind her. "I didn't become a cheerleader. You're a queen bee now. I'm still just a drone."

"Oh, Anna." She sighs. "This isn't Animal Planet." Now she just sounds patronizing. "Cheerleading isn't all glitz and glamour, you know. It's hard work."

I open my mouth, full of sarcastic comebacks, but before I can pick one she says, "You seem . . . happy. I mean, not that you were miserable before, but you seem to be having more fun . . . with your new friends."

"So you're saying you did me a favor," I say, trying not to smile, "by dumping me?"

"No." Dani sounds slightly miffed and also slightly embarrassed. "That's not what I'm saying."

"Okay."

"I miss you sometimes," she says quietly. "That's all."

"You do?"

"Yeah."

Anyone can surprise you, I guess, if you wait long enough. You can even surprise yourself. "I miss you sometimes, too."

Ethan groans. "You girls give me the shits. Drama, drama, drama."

I'm pretty sure he means this as an insult, but I don't take it that way. I laugh. He looks at me, surprised. When he smiles, I swear his eyes change color.

Maybe Ethan Zane is a witch . . . . or whatever the male equivalent is . . . a warlock? The thought makes me laugh again, under my breath. I can't wait to tell Nicole and Chloe.

*   *   *

"Try this one," Marnie says. I am sitting at the kitchen counter after school, surrounded by muffins. "It's pumpkin spice."

"Mmm," I say with my mouth full.

"I know, right?" Marnie says. Then, to Jane, who is sitting in her high chair, playing with a spoon, "Pumpkin is full of antioxidants, Janie. Can you say *an-ti-ox-i-dants*?"

Jane blows a raspberry like she thinks Marnie is full of crap.

"That's right, *antioxidants*."

Marnie still bugs me with her baby talk, but it's hard to be annoyed with her for long. She is so fired up about this Marnie's Muffins thing. It's sort of contagious. The other night, when I came in after my big talk with my dad, and I told her congratulations—not for being pregnant, but for starting a baking business—she said, "I have you to thank, Anna."

"You have *Cupcake Wars* to thank," I said.

"No." She shook her head. "You made the kale cupcakes comment. That's what got me thinking."

"I was mocking you a little. Sorry."

"I know you were mocking me. And I forgive you. Because you're *also* the one who suggested I go back to work, which is what made me decide to do this."

"I am?"

"On the plane, remember? On our way home from Atlanta."

"Well," I said, "glad to be of service."

One of these days, I may have to tell her that "Marnie's Muffins" is a stupid name for a business, and I think she can come up with something better. But I won't say it now. She is too jazzed about these pumpkin spice minimuffins.

I pick up another. "I think," I say, "that you should

call this one the Clemson Tiger. Because it's such a lovely shade of orange."

"Oh, Anna."

"Am I right?"

"You are so right."

CHAPTER
24

MARNIE IS COOKING for Thanksgiving, and I am a little afraid. Not just about the food, but about the cast of characters. Besides my dad, Jane, and me, Marnie has invited Shawna and her mom, Regina and my mom, and Mr. Pfaff.

No, I am not kidding.

Yes, I am gobsmacked.

Marnie and my mother have only been in the same room twice. Once after Jane was born, when my mom brought me to the hospital to meet her. And once when my mom dropped me off at my dad's one Saturday morning and Marnie asked if she wanted to come in for a cup of tea. Both times, it was so awkward I wanted to run away screaming. But does that stop Marnie from inviting my mother for Thanksgiving? No.

Marnie and I are in Whole Foods, doing the big shop. This will not be your typical American Thanksgiving with stuffing and candied yams. Oh no. This will be what Marnie calls a "historically accurate, authentic Pilgrim feast." We're talking wildfowl. We're talking corn porridge. We're talking chestnuts, venison, shellfish. Last weekend, my father even built a fire pit in the backyard, so the meat can be "spit roasted" before it goes into the oven.

Marnie's cart is already loaded up with organic, locally grown onions, beans, lettuce, spinach, cabbage, and carrots. I have the list and I'm checking things off as we go.

"We only want fruits indigenous to the region," Marnie announces, grabbing a carton of blueberries off a shelf. "Plums." She throws a few in the cart. "Cranberries." She grabs a bag. "So . . . what do you think about this friend of your mother's? Peter, is it?"

"You mean Mr. Pfaff, my *teacher*? How can this possibly be good?"

Marnie smiles. "Maybe you'll get an easy A."

"Oh, please!" I say. I think about all the blank papers I've handed in. Then, "I can't believe she asked if she could invite him."

"It's Thanksgiving." Marnie throws some grapes in the cart. "The more the merrier. Who knows . . . maybe they'll hit it off."

"They're just friends," I say firmly. "They knew each other a million years ago."

"Stranger things have happened," Marnie says. "Your father and I barely knew each other at all. We fell in love in two hours. He asked me to marry him after six weeks."

I groan. That's just what I need, my mother falling in love with Mr. Pfaff. Instead of watching TV together, we'll be reading the dictionary aloud every night.

"No one should be alone on Thanksgiving," Marnie says. She looks around. "Now, where are the gooseberries?"

Gooseberries. Elderberries. Mussels. Marnie will be cooking all day to get ready for tomorrow. I've offered to help, but she says she wants to do it all herself.

Have I mentioned that this will be an authentic Pilgrim feast? Have I mentioned the fire pit? Have I mentioned that I'm nervous?

*   *   *

Shawna and her mom are the first to arrive. They are both wearing dresses, and Shawna, for the first time since I've known her, has drawn her eyebrows where eyebrows actually grow. Instead of daggers, they are gentle arches. Instead of black, they are brown.

"Oh my God," I say. "You look—"

"Shut up," she says, poking me with a serving spoon.

"I was going to say *pretty*."

"Isn't she?" Shawna's mom smiles at me. She looks like Shawna, with nice crinkles around her eyes and a big ceramic bowl in her arms. "Where can I put this fruit salad?"

I point her in the direction of the kitchen.

"Thanks for inviting us," Shawna says, giving my shoulder a punch. She tells me about the latest drama: her dad wanted her for half the day today, but her mom said no because he gets her on Christmas, so they had a screaming fight on the phone, and he threatened to take Shawna's mother to court all over again.

"I'm sorry," I say.

Shawna shrugs. "What're ya gonna do?"

"Mocktail?" I say, handing her one of the drinks I made for us in the kitchen: cranberry juice and seltzer with little paper umbrellas sticking out the top.

"Fancy," Shawna says.

"Only the best for this awkward gathering."

"It may not be so awkward."

I give her a look. "Do I really need to spell this out? . . . There's my father and his twenty-four-year-old wife, who, by the way, is cooking *venison* out in the *fire pit* . . . there's his bipolar ex-wife, and *her* old friend, my *English teacher* . . . there's a screaming baby and there's Regina's big mouth. No, this won't be awkward at all."

Shawna nods. "Point taken."

A few minutes later, Regina arrives, carrying wine and meatballs. "Anna Banana! I'd hug you if I had a free arm!" She's followed by my mom, who's wearing a blue dress I've never seen before. It nips in at the waist and hugs her hips just right.

"You look good, Mom," I say.

"Thanks, honey."

When she gives me a kiss I smell cigarettes, which kind of bums me out. I want to say, *Really, Mom?* But I guess her being here is enough. That and the look on Mr. Pfaff's face when he walks up the front path. He takes one look at that blue dress and stops, bug-eyed, the flowers in his hand wavering a little.

"Hi, Peter," she says, smiling.

"Fran. Wow."

"Hi, Mr. Pfaff," I say.

"Anna." He drags his eyes away from my mom long enough to hand me one of the bouquets. "Happy Thanksgiving."

"Thank you," I say. The flowers are pretty, all autumn colors.

There's an awkward moment in the foyer, when

Marnie and my dad and Shawna's mom all come rushing to meet everyone. Shawna and I take this opportunity to sneak upstairs, thinking that if we wait until the adults have had some wine, maybe by the time we go down they will be nice and relaxed.

We play Tiny Wings on our phones. We text Sarabeth, Chloe, Nicole, and Reese. We listen to music. We are just about to put on "Crazy Dreams," when we hear a voice from downstairs. A single voice, at first. It sounds like Marnie yelling, *Crap! Crap! Crap!* Now there's shrieking. Jane, I think.

There's a lot of commotion. A door banging, a pot slamming, and then laughter. My mother? I know that laugh. Oh, God, what has she done this time?

I look at Shawna and we both start running down the stairs. We run into the kitchen just as the smoke alarm goes off. Marnie is swearing, my mother is laughing, and the wildfowl is sitting in the middle of the floor.

"What the—" I come to a screeching halt.

"It's a comedy of errors!" Regina yells over the noise.

My dad is jabbing the smoke detector with a broom handle. Mr. Pfaff is holding a shrieking Jane. Shawna's mom is opening windows. My mother and Marnie are now squatting over the wildfowl, attempting to lift it with the tiny woven potholders I made in third grade.

Shawna's mouth gapes open. "How did—"

"Dropped on the transfer!" Regina yells. "Rookie mistake!"

The smoke alarm goes silent. Marnie and my mother heave the wildfowl up and onto a platter. They're both flushed and splattered with grease. My mother gives a whoop of triumph. Jane stops crying long enough to hiccup. Marnie looks dazed, a clump of hair stuck to her face.

"It's ruined," she says softly.

"It's not ruined," my mother says.

"I killed the bird."

"I'm pretty sure it was already dead," Regina says.

My mother gives Regina a pointed look. "It's fine."

"It's dirty," Marnie says.

My mom puts an arm around her, which just about stuns me. I feel like I am witnessing a miracle right here in my father's kitchen. It doesn't seem that long ago that she could barely look at Marnie. Now she's hugging her and telling her that the wildfowl is still edible.

"A little dirt never hurt," Shawna's mother pipes in.

And Mr. Pfaff adds, "Good for the immune system." He looks strangely comfortable holding a baby. He keeps tickling Jane's belly and she keeps tipping her head back and giggling.

Marnie shakes her head. "I wanted this dinner to be perfect."

"Perfection is overrated," my mother says firmly.

Then, to my dad, "Remember, David, our first Thanksgiving? I forgot to put the turkey in a pan?"

"Oh yes," my dad says.

Marnie sort of smiles. "How could you forget a pan?"

"I don't know," my mom says. "I'd never cooked a turkey before. I just stuck it in the oven."

"She started a grease fire," my dad says. "The fire department came."

Marnie's eyes widen. "The fire department came?"

"It did." My dad smiles.

"Did you eat the turkey?"

"Inedible. Charred beyond recognition."

"Will you eat this one?"

"Yes," he says, simply. Nothing else. And then they kiss.

"Okay, okay," Regina says. "Are we gonna carve this dirty bird or what?"

*   *   *

After dinner, we sit around the fire pit in the backyard. The air is cold and crisp. Marnie passes around sweatshirts for everyone. Shawna and her mom huddle together under a blanket. Mr. Pfaff and my dad take turns stoking the fire like a couple of cavemen. Regina lounges on a beach chair with Jane in her lap, drinking a beer.

"All we need is sticks!" Marnie says, holding up a bag of marshmallows. This is her one concession to an otherwise authentic Pilgrim feast: marshmallows. She says it was a tradition in her family when she was young. They always roasted marshmallows on Thanksgiving.

"Come on." My mom gives my sleeve a tug. "Anna and I are going on a stick hunt."

So we walk into the woods. We need to find eight marshmallow sticks. The leaves crackle under our feet. My mom slips a little in her dress shoes. We stop in front of a big dead branch with lots of long skinny branches attached. We each break one off.

"So how are you, Anna?" my mother says quietly. "Tell me how you're feeling these days." She stands there in one of my dad's old sweatshirts, half lit by the moon.

"Tell me how *you're* feeling these days."

"I'm feeling . . ." She breaks a few twiggy pieces off her branch. "Okay. Pretty good, actually."

I wonder how much of "pretty good" is the medication and how much is her telling me what I want to hear. I wonder how long "pretty good" will last. I could ask, but I know she won't be able to promise anything. And anyway, I don't want to ruin the night. The mood is too good.

I can see the fire through the trees. Crackling and sparking, lighting up everyone's face. Maybe we can have a campout here, in the spring. Me, Shawna, Sara-beth, Chloe, Nicole, and Reese. If I'm still living here—or even if I'm not. Who knows where you'll find me in the next six months? Maybe my mom will stay on her meds. Maybe she won't. Maybe my dad will get custody. Maybe I'll get a beanbag couch. Maybe Marnie's Muffins will take off. Maybe she'll get pregnant. I don't know. But I have to believe that whatever smacks me in the face next, I can handle. Maybe I'll even smack it back. Mean-while, there are marshmallows to roast.

"Come on," I say.

We gather our sticks. When my mom stumbles a little on a root, I catch her arm. We loop our elbows together and walk out of the woods.

ACKNOWLEDGMENTS

THANKS AND HUGS TO:

My remarkable editor, Joy Peskin, whose well of positive feedback never runs dry, and who has assured me that, if all else fails, I will have a bright future naming pharmaceutical drugs.

My *extremely* patient literary agent, Rebecca Sherman, for waiting ten years.

The Clemson sorority girls in my Intro to Rhetoric and Argument class, for bringing Marnie to life.

The nuns of Nonneberg Abbey, especially Sister Berthe, Sister Sophia, and Sister Stein, who kept me laughing—and harmonizing—during the final stages of this book.

Everyone I ever dragged into one of my talent show acts, for being awesome.

Julie, my neighbor and dear friend, for appreciating the pillbox hat.

My dad, for the brooms he sold to buy me that orange typewriter.

My husband, the business guru, for "paradigm shift," "benchmarking," and "value added," and for his unwavering support.

Jack, Ben, and Emma, for lighting the way.

My mom, for being the strongest person I know. I love you.

RESOURCES

IF YOU THINK YOUR PARENT might be clinically depressed, begin by talking to a trusted adult—a relative, a teacher, or a school counselor—about what's been going on.

If you're worried that your parent is suicidal, call one of these twenty-four-hour, totally confidential telephone hotlines:

National Suicide Prevention Lifeline
1-800-273-TALK (8255)
1-800-784-2433

Covenant House Nineline
1-800-999-9999

Boys Town Hotline
1-800-448-3000

Remember, depression and other types of mental illness are treatable. This is not about blame. This is not about being a "bad parent." The sooner you ask for help, the sooner your mom or dad can get treatment.

GO FISH

QUESTIONS FOR THE AUTHOR

NATASHA FRIEND

What did you want to be when you grew up?
An Olympic gymnast.

When did you realize you wanted to be a writer?
At age six, as soon as I could read.

What's your most embarrassing childhood memory?
Riding my bike into a school bus in front of the boy I had a crush on.

What's your favorite childhood memory?
Playing baseball in the park with my dad.

As a young person, who did you look up to most?
Mary Lou Retton and Judy Blume.

What was your favorite thing about school?
Writing!

What were your hobbies as a kid?
Reading, singing, acting, playing the piano, climbing trees, riding my bike.

What are your hobbies now?
Reading, cheering on my kids, holding spontaneous dance parties in the kitchen.

Did you play sports as a kid?
Lots! Gymnastics, field hockey, basketball, softball, soccer.

What was your first job, and what was your "worst" job?
My first job was babysitting and my worst job, by far, was picking strawberries.

What book is on your nightstand now?
Carry On, Warrior by Glennon Doyle Melton.

How did you celebrate publishing your first book?
Ice cream and lots of dancing for joy.

Where do you write your books?
In my office overlooking the lake in my backyard.

What sparked your imagination for *Where You'll Find Me*?
My relationship with my mom, who has battled bipolar disorder her whole life.

What challenges do you face in the writing process?
Time! I have three kids, so there's never enough time in the day for anything.

What is your favorite word?
Mellifluous.

If you could live in any fictional place, what would it be?
Hogwarts.

Who is your favorite fictional character?
Pippi Longstocking.

What was your favorite book when you were a kid?
Are You There, God? It's Me, Margaret by Judy Blume.

Do you have a favorite book now?
My favorite book is always the one I'm currently writing.

If you could travel in time, where would you go and what would you do?
I would go back to age thirteen, knowing what I know now. I would stand up to all the people who made me feel small and worthless.

What's the best advice you have ever received about writing?
Show; don't tell.

What advice do you wish someone had given you when you were younger?
Be brave. Take risks.

Do you ever get writer's block?
I can't afford writer's block because my writing time is so limited, but when I do feel stuck, I read. Reading great books always inspires me.

What do you want readers to remember about your books?
Laughing and crying. Hopefully I can make my readers do both.

What would you do if you ever stopped writing?
I'd buy a summer camp in Maine and be a camp director until I was too old to paddle a canoe.

If you were a superhero, what would your superpower be?
Hosting talent shows.

Do you have any strange or funny habits?
I can speak a secret language called Oppy. Everyone in my family can.

Did you have any strange or funny habits when you were a kid?
I used to walk up and down the stairs on my hands.

What do you consider to be your greatest accomplishment?
My three children.

What would your readers be most surprised to learn about you?
I don't mind people thinking I'm weird. When I was younger, I wanted to be normal. The older I get, the more comfortable I am being different.

A fresh and funny story about two teens conceived via in vitro fertilization who go in search of answers about their donor, and discover the true meaning of the other F-word: *family*.

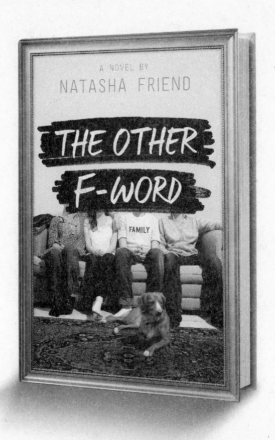

KEEP READING FOR AN EXCERPT.

HOLLIS

THE PICTURE OF PAM HANGING OVER THE FIREPLACE WAS like the portrait of Phineas Nigellus hanging over the headmaster's desk at Hogwarts. Watching. Judging. Pam was a perpetual presence, a denim-clad specter presiding over the suckfest that was Hollis Darby-Barnes's life.

Pam's eyes: the golden brown of a Siberian tiger.

Hollis's eyes: the brown of a dung beetle.

Pam's hair: the neat, feathered cap of an Olympic skater from the 1980s.

Hollis's hair: a blender experiment. Bon Jovi, the perm years.

Hollis wanted to rip Pam off the wall and throw her into the fireplace. Also, she wanted to throw Pam's cat into the fireplace. Pam's cat was named Yvette. She was fifteen—exactly a year older than Hollis—but unlike

Hollis, she had white, fluffy hair, a smashed-in face, and a problem with fur balls.

Hollis hardly remembered Pam. She wasn't biologically related to Pam. She felt no emotional connection to Pam whatsoever. And yet Hollis's mother continued to insist that Hollis share Pam's last name, Barnes. This, among a million other things, pissed Hollis off.

It pissed Hollis off that her mother still wore Pam's bathrobe. It pissed Hollis off that her mother referred to Pam as Hollis's "mom." It pissed Hollis off that even though Pam died seven years ago, her mother had yet to go on a single date. Worse than anything, it pissed Hollis off that her mother maintained Pam's Hotmail account. Because A) Pam was dead, and B) who the hell had a Hotmail account?

"Why?" Hollis would ask her mother every time she placed an order on Amazon as PjBarnesie_373@hotmail .com.

Her mother always gave the same answer: "Pam was the love of my life. It makes me feel better to know she's still here."

"But she's *not* still here," Hollis would say.

"When a package arrives with Pam's name on it, I feel like she is."

It was a freaking losing battle. Did Hollis want Pam's memory hanging around their house like a bad smell? No, she did not. But what could she do? Her mother was all she had. Leigh Darby wasn't a bad mom as mothers went. She didn't do drugs. She didn't bring perverts home from bars. She didn't dress like a stripper. She made good money as a real estate agent. Every morning, Hollis's mother got up, took a shower, blew her hair straight, and put on a pantsuit. She poured cereal for Hollis. She went out into the world, smiled, and said things like "cozy three-bedroom" and "granite countertops."

Then she came home, put on Pam's bathrobe, and talked to the picture above the fireplace. "My feet are killing me, babe." Or, "Guess what, babe? I made a sale today!" Would Hollis's mother ever take Pam down and move on with her life? No, Hollis was certain she wouldn't. Even four years from now, when Hollis left for college, her mother would still be here, festering. So would Yvette, no doubt. That cat refused to die.

God, it was pathetic. Even more pathetic than the fact that today was December thirty-first and Hollis had no plans whatsoever for New Year's Eve.

"Honey?"

Hollis looked up from her cereal bowl. She gave her mother a blank stare.

"Pam just got an email."

This depressed Hollis even more. And pissed her off. "You know dead people can't get email, right?"

"It's from Milo Robinson-Clark."

Okay, wait. "What?"

Hollis's mother smiled. "Milo Robinson-Clark is trying to get in touch with you."

Milo Robinson-Clark. Milo Robinson-Clark. Why does that name sound— Oh God. Lodged in Hollis's mind was the image of a little dark-haired boy on the other end of a seesaw. Train conductor overalls. A red juice mustache.

"That kid we met when Pam—"

Hollis's mother nodded vigorously. "That's right."

"What were his moms'—?"

"Suzanne and Frankie."

"Right," Hollis muttered. Then, "Jesus."

Milo Robinson-Clark emailed a dead woman. He emailed a dead woman to contact the girl he met once, a million years ago, on the other end of a seesaw. This made no sense. It only made sense if he didn't know Pam was dead, and even then—

"How does that make you feel?" her mother asked. She sounded like the stupid grief counselor Hollis had been forced to see after Pam died. *Draw a picture of your feelings, Hollis. Use this puppet to have a conversation, Hollis. How does that make you feel, Hollis?*

How did Hollis feel about her sperm donor's son suddenly popping up in Pam's Hotmail inbox? She felt weird, that's how she felt. She felt weird all over. Hollis barely remembered meeting Milo Robinson-Clark. She'd been, what, six years old? There was a photo somewhere.

The whole thing had been Pam's idea. Right after her ovarian cancer diagnosis, Pam had tracked down Milo's moms through some lesbian life partner/sperm donor website. Hollis wasn't exactly sure how it worked, except that sperm donors had ID numbers, and her donor's ID number and Milo's donor's ID number matched, so that's how Pam and Leigh and Suzanne and Frankie found each other. The four moms had conducted a reunion of sorts. There was a playground. A picnic. Hollis vaguely remembered brownies.

And then Pam got sick, like really fast, and that was the end of that. Because Hollis's mother was swept up in caring for Pam and then she was swept up in grieving for Pam, and Hollis never saw her half brother again.

Half brother. God.

Hollis was struck, once more, by the bizarre nature of her existence. Most of the time she just futzed along through life—going to school, doing her homework, eating and sleeping and reading—and then, out of nowhere, a lightning bolt would strike.

I was conceived in a petri dish.

My father is out there.

I have a half brother.

"Jesus," Hollis muttered again. "Why does he want to get in touch with me?"

Her mother shook her head. "He doesn't say."

"He *doesn't say*?"

"I have it right here."

"What?"

Her mother held up a piece of paper. "The email. I printed it out."

Hollis felt her stomach tense.

"'Dear Pam,'" her mother began reading, with no regard. "'My name is Milo Robinson-Clark.'"

No forethought.

"'I got your email from my mom Suzanne.'"

Still no indication whatsoever from Hollis that she wanted to hear this.

"'You may not remember me, but we met seven and a half years ago in Brooklyn, where I still live. Your daughter, Hollis, and I have the same sperm donor. Which is actually why I'm writing. I'm hoping you'll pass this message along to Hollis and tell her that I'd like to hear from her. She can email or text or call me, whatever works. Or I can email or text or call her, if you send me her info. Thanks. Hope you and Leigh are both well. Milo.'" Hollis's mother looked up. "So?"

Hollis stared at her.

"What do you think?"

"What do I *think*?"

"Do you . . ." Her mother hesitated. "Would you like me to give him your email address or your cell phone number so he can contact you?"

Hollis picked up her spoon and shoved a massive bite of Froot Loops into her mouth. Chewed, swallowed, shoved in another bite. "Whatever," she said finally, spraying cereal chunks onto the table.

Hollis's mother hated the word *whatever*. She called it a passive-aggressive conversation-blocking tool, but this time she didn't comment. This time, for some crazy reason, she took it to mean, *Do whatever you want*. Which is why, ten hours later—when Hollis's mother went to pick up Chinese food and Hollis was lying in her bed, staring at the ceiling—Hollis's phone pinged from the pocket of her hoodie.

She checked: area code 917. She read: **Hey. It's Milo.**

Hollis almost laughed. It was such a casual text, like they weren't on a hyphenated-last-name basis. Like it wasn't completely absurd and random for her sperm donor's other kid to suddenly be contacting her when they only met once, a million years ago, on a seesaw in Brooklyn.

Hey, Hollis texted back anyway.

Happy almost new year.

To u too.

How r u?

Ok.

How r your moms?

Um Leighs good. Pams dead tho.

O shit. I didn't know.

No biggie. It was 7 years ago.

It occurred to Hollis that it was rude of her mother not to let Suzanne and Frankie know that Pam had died. Because, well, wasn't there some protocol for informing your biological daughter's half brother's lesbian moms that your own lesbian partner was dead?

Hollis stifled a snort. This was so *weird*.

I know this is weird, Milo Robinson-Clark texted.

Hollis was so spooked she sat up. It was like he had read her mind or something, which clearly he hadn't, because how could he read her mind? It's not weird.

No?

No.

Well it's about to get weird cuz I have something to tell u.

Ok.

R u ready?

Yes.

I've decided to find r sperm donor.

Breath caught in Hollis's throat. She stared at her phone. She read the text again just to make sure she'd read it right. Then she exhaled. Y?

Medical reasons.

R u ok?

Yes.

Do u need a kidney?

No.

Bone marrow?

No.

???

It's complicated.

Hollis waited. If Milo Robinson-Clark wanted to tell her about his mysterious medical condition, he would. And apparently he did not, because his next text read,

R u in?

In?

For finding r donor?

Okay, wait. WTF. Hollis's heart was suddenly pounding so fast she needed to lie back down. She tried not to think about this. She tried not to let these thoughts infiltrate her mind. *I am a freak of nature. I am a lab experiment. I am only half a person.* Most of the time she succeeded. But sometimes, just sometimes, she fantasized about tracking down her donor, setting up a time and a place to meet, and then—right after she said "Hi, I'm Hollis"—slapping him across the face.

Because Hollis was pissed at the guy. She didn't even know him and she was pissed. Even if he did donate out of the goodness of his heart to help lesbians make babies. The way Hollis was "made" was fast, cold, and impersonal. Her existence had nothing to do with love. And if you're not going to make a baby out of love, at least have a one-night stand with some hot stranger you met at the Laundromat. At least then there's human contact. A connection between two people. It isn't fair to just go and squirt your jiz in a cup, take your cash, and then not even *think* about where your DNA is going and who might be affected.

Hollis's phone pinged. **Pls? I don't want to do this alone.**

Milo Robinson-Clark did not want to find their sperm donor alone. He wanted Hollis to join him. He was offering her a chance—a once-in-a-lifetime opportunity to meet her genetic father, to have all of her unanswered questions answered. Hollis would be crazy not to take it, wouldn't she?

But no, hell no, sorry, no. The anger that was usually just simmering beneath the surface of Hollis's skin now rose like a tidal wave, taking all good things with it.

I'm out.

Hollis texted the words. Then, for good measure, she chucked her phone across the room and cracked a picture frame. Which made her feel a little better. But not much.